Dear Diary,

It's 3:00 a.m. and I can't get a wink of sleep. How can I—now that Ross has stormed back into my life without warning? Has it really been three years? Three years since I last felt his heated gaze burn through my soul...three years since I succumbed to the power of his electrifying embrace? Not a day has gone by that I haven't yearned for Ross—or wished I could rewrite history. But the past is the past and Ross isn't about to forgive me for all the pain I've caused him. If only he knew how I really felt about him. If only he'd look at me like he used to—with deep love and abiding trust. Now every time I glance into his intense brown eyes, all I can see is anger and bitterness. And passion. But passion was never the problem. The desire we feel for each other is more intoxicating than ever. Yet I won't surrender to him on his terms. After all, what is the point of lovemaking without emotional tenderness? And if there's a chance that I can get Ross to love me again, I'll fight for a future with him. After all, I love this infuriating, dynamic, utterly unforgettable man with all my heart....

FAMILY

FAMILY

Ann MAJOR

Love Me Again

12
9   MARRIED
    FOR A   3
    MINUTE
    6

Silhouette Books

Published by Silhouette Books

America's Publisher of Contemporary Romance

SILHOUETTE BOOKS
300 East 42nd St.,
New York, N.Y. 10017

ISBN 0-373-82170-0

LOVE ME AGAIN

Copyright © 1983 by Ann Major

This edition published by arrangement with Harlequin Books S.A.

® and TM are trademarks of Harlequin Books S.A., used under license. Trademarks indicated with ® are registered in the United States Patent and Trademark Office, the Canadian Trade Marks Office and in other countries.

Visit us at www.romance.net

Printed in U.S.A.

Dear Reader,

This story was written for all the women in the world who've loved and lost, who've struggled with regrets too painful to reveal, who've wished there was some way to say "I'm sorry," but find it's too late.

Life goes on. Broken hearts mend. If we're lucky, we let go and forge new lives. But some of us never forget those special people who taught us lessons when we were too young to learn.

We are carried past points of no return. This book was my way of saying I'm sorry to someone who taught me the value of love. I didn't appreciate this person until it was too late. Partly because of this relationship, I will never take love for granted again.

With this book, I celebrate all loves—those lost and those found. Each love is a special kind of miracle.

Sincerely,

Ann Major

Please address questions and book requests to:
Silhouette Reader Service
U.S.: 3010 Walden Ave., P.O. Box 1325, Buffalo, NY 14269
Canadian: P.O. Box 609, Fort Erie, Ont. L2A 5X3

Especially for the three young people who
have added immeasurably to my own life—
David, Kimberley and Tad, my beloved children.

Escape! The single word had flashed through her mind the moment her eyes had accidentally met Ross's deep dark amber gaze across the crush of people that had separated them. Instantly she'd forgotten the thick acrid smoke that was almost choking her, the dense press of warm human flesh that constantly jogged against her body as people moved to and from the bar sloshing drinks crazily, the vibrant loud clatter of too many voices shouting over hard rock in order to be heard. In that split second of frozen time before Ross's expression had blackened and he'd torn his eyes from her pain-glazed face, a million memories from the past had attacked her, some of them excruciating in their intensity.

For an instant she'd seen a vision of Tami's still, white face, her delicate heart-shaped mouth blue, her amber lashes forever closed. Ross knelt by the shell drive of their former home and cradled her small body in his arms for the last time before the ambulance tore toward their house, the wail of its siren screaming ever louder along the normally silent forest road, its blare drowning out the sounds of her own aching sobs. She'd stood wordlessly beside Ross beneath the gigantic cypress trees, her high heels sinking into the spongy earth and lawn that grew near the bayou.

But other memories had been surprisingly warm and gentle. She'd remembered that first thrilling moment Ross had seen her as a child no longer, but as a willowy beauty he desired. On their first date Ross had given her a single bloodred rose, and when she'd brushed the fragile blossom with her lips, the petals had still been warm from the touch of his fingers. She'd remembered the tenderness and hunger of their first embrace under a full moon that had sent silver fingers of light sifting through the towering pines of the dense jungle-forest of southeast Texas—the lumber country of which Ross and her own father were kings. Those memories made her ache with a nostalgic yearning, and she'd felt fresh sorrow that this man who'd once loved her so completely could no longer bear the sight of her.

Why this race of panic now? She'd thought she was over Ross, and the spell of his virile masculine self. She'd thought that grief and bitterness had obliterated all the finer feelings they'd once shared. Hadn't she told herself that that part of her life was behind her, where she wanted it to be?

Diana shivered violently and clutched with one hand at the edges of the gauzy black point-lace ruffle that served as a wrap about her shoulders, then threw open the glass door with the other and stepped outside onto the balcony. She felt strangely dizzy as she leaned heavily against the railing, and normally she would have thought it was the sheer drop beneath her or the summer heat that made her feel faint.

She was scarcely aware of the door sliding shut behind her, its closing muting the throbbing beat of the band and the din of the revelers inside. Nor did she see the glamorous glitter of a million lights twinkling from the brashly new ultramodern buildings soaring around her, each skyscraper more lavish in conception than the one constructed only months before, enormous thrusts of steel and brick that had sprung up almost overnight amidst the fabulous wealth of Houston's southwest. She was wrapped in her own world of pain and loss, and she had to blink rapidly against the tears that threatened to fall. Roughly she brushed at her eyes with the back of her hand, not caring that she might smudge her carefully applied makeup.

She realized suddenly in a quick piercing sensation that nothing in her life mattered to her except Ross. Not her meteoric success in business, her list of prominent clients, the eligible bachelors who routinely escorted her to a never-ending weekend round of lavish parties that she attended to make valuable contacts. She had a closet filled with designer clothes, a penthouse condominium in one of southwest Houston's most prestigious neighborhoods. She had all that money and success could buy, and yet at the center of it all—her soul—there was the most terrible emptiness.

She was a fool—to have realized this tonight, instead of three years ago! She'd destroyed her marriage with reckless deliberateness, rationalizing her actions by convincing herself that their relationship had been impossible from the beginning, that even if there hadn't been Tami and what had happened, she and Ross had been too different to make their marriage work. She'd been born to wealth and a life of ease while Ross, a rugged outdoorsman, a tough executive in the lumber business, was a self-made man. Born of poor Louisiana bayou people, he had not wanted the glittering life-style she'd thought was so important, even after he'd become a successful man. He'd tried to persuade her that she didn't, either, telling her that she only thought she did because it was what her mother, Madelaine, wanted for her, and expected. Sometimes, deep down, Diana had almost believed Ross.

Quickly she pushed thoughts of Madelaine from her mind. Instead she remembered the rustic, two-story home nestled deep in the piney woods of East Texas that she and Ross had shared. The house was built on the lush bank of a quietly flowing bayou. Ross had loved their home, the simplicity of it, the wildness of the bayou, the cypress trees veiled with the floating gray draperies of Spanish moss and the haunting wilderness of the woods. He'd built the house himself and had never understood why Diana would have preferred a more elegant home near the country club. "Those houses are all alike," he would say. "They're exactly like your parents' house. Ours is unique; it's ours alone."

Well, she'd lost Ross, their home, Tami—her whole world—and moved away to Houston and built a new life for herself, a successful, satisfying life, she'd told herself too often. And now, in one shattering moment, Diana saw that for three years she'd been deluding herself, for without Ross nothing mattered.

Nothing except Adam, she corrected herself quickly. She still had her adopted ten-year-old son— at least some of the time. She smiled fleetingly, the

curve of her lips softening her beautiful, slender face.
Adam was the one thing that made her life worth-
while, now that she had lost everything else. He was
Ross's son by his first marriage, and she had legally
adopted him when she'd married Ross eight years before.

Ross allowed him to visit her frequently, even
though he himself never brought him or even talked
to Diana on the phone to make arrangements. Madelaine was their intermediary. Adam had just completed a four-week summer visit, and Diana had
driven him to camp, neutral territory, from which
Ross would pick him up in a week and take him home
to Orange.

Her smile lingered, as it always did when she
thought of Adam. He was tall for his age, and every
day he looked more like his father. He was as dark
as an Indian after a month at the pool and the beach
in Galveston, his raven hair bleached auburn at the
temples. Yesterday Diana had been so proud of
Adam. He'd stood straight as an arrow like a little
soldier in his crisp uniform as he'd waved good-bye
to her at that smotheringly hot, primitive boy scout
camp on the lush banks of Lake Conroe, north of
Houston. She'd thought him the most handsome of
all the boys, and she'd almost been the last mother to
leave, even though she'd been thankful she could
climb back into her air-conditioned car and drive
away to civilized comfort. But she already missed
him, and she worried about him out there.

Diana's thoughts drifted back to the tall, rugged

man inside whose sudden and unexpected appearance had churned her emotions with the ruthless violence of a tornado. What was Ross doing here tonight, she wondered desperately. She knew, of course, that had he had the slightest idea she might be here, he would never have come. For three years they had taken the greatest pains to avoid each other.

It was a hot July night, and eighteen stories beneath her Houston sprawled—beautiful in the darkness, fiercely bold and brash, ablaze with night lights and steaming with heat. But she didn't even look down, and even if she had, she couldn't have seen it through the shimmering haze of her tears. Her thoughts were on the man inside—her husband—and the shock of seeing him again after three years.

Not a breath of air stirred the impractically sexy gown she was wearing. Whispers of sheer black cloth clung to her slender body and accentuated her surprisingly shapely curves, enhancing the soft honey tones of her flesh.

Diana was beautiful, but not in the ordinary voluptuous manner. There was a quality about her that was arresting. When she entered a room, all eyes turned in her direction, although when people told her so, she always laughed in disbelief, the velvet sound of her warm laughter as ingenuous as the woman herself.

She was tall—too tall, she'd always thought—delicate of bone and graceful in movement. She looked conspicuously different from the rest of her relatives, who were all short and chunky. Clothes, even jeans and a blouse, looked magnificent on her lean, supple body. She could have been a model, had she had the slightest desire to pursue such a career. But her other, more artistic, talents had won out, and she'd majored in interior design in college.

Diana's satiny black hair fell in thick, lush waves many inches past her shoulders. The rich creamy glow of her skin was smooth against her dark hair, and she appeared much younger than her thirty years. She had large blue eyes, starred with thick bristly dark lashes. Her enormous eyes in her narrow face gave her the innocent look of a startled young doe. Her lips were full and moist, promising sensuality. Her innate sense of style enabled her to make the most of her striking looks. But it was the inner warmth of her personality that lighted her features and transformed her into a radiant beauty. There was about her an aura of softness and vulnerability that made men, caught in her spell, want to protect her. And tonight in her chic, daringly sexy gown she was unquestionably alluring.

The rush of refrigerated air and the whir of the glass door sliding in its track behind her caught her off guard, and she jumped slightly. The wild, beating music blared loudly for an instant before the glass door clicked shut once more. She caught the scent of familiar cologne and turned.

"Oh, Bruce...." She smiled weakly in nervous relief and reached for his arm. The feel of his strength beneath his pale silk coat sleeve was only slightly reassuring, but she clung to him anyway.

"I missed you," he said, his deep voice full of

kindly regard. His silver hair gleamed in the soft light. In the darkness the lines beneath his eyes were invisible, and she realized how awesomely handsome he must have been twenty years ago. Even at sixty he was still an attractive man.

Bruce was her rock. He owned the condominium next to hers, and they'd met two years ago at the building swimming pool. Since that time they'd become devoted friends, neither of them wanting anything more from their relationship. Bruce had a ten-year-old grandson, Robby, who visited his grandfather in the summers when Adam did. The two boys were great friends, and Diana and Bruce enjoyed taking them places together. Only last Saturday evening the four of them had gone out to Astroworld to ride the roller coaster, the Texas Cyclone.

That Diana and Bruce's friendship caused speculation and envy among the numerous older single females in their building gave neither of them the slightest concern. In fact it often afforded Bruce a hearty laugh. "I'm just vain enough to get a kick out of having a beauty around like you to flaunt—when the need arises," he'd said once, his gray eyes twinkling with humor as he'd stared down at Diana lounging beside him at the pool in her string bikini while an attractive dowager who'd pestered him with several invitations stared daggers through them both.

Bruce was a widower who had married briefly on the rebound several years before. His second wife had married him because of his fabulous wealth, and now that he was single again he was very cautious where women were concerned. "Too cautious," Diana often chided him affectionately. And he would reply sagely, "No more than you, my dear."

For that she had no comeback. It was common knowledge that she had no interest in men. Bruce teased her about this, occasionally saying this was why so many men were interested in her. "You're a relief from a world filled with man-hungry, desperate divorcées," he would say with more than a little truth. And Diana would laugh brittlely.

Diana didn't care whether men found her attractive or unattractive. That part of her life belonged to another time. Besides, she wasn't divorced—legally. Just before she and Ross had separated, as his last act of gallantry, he'd told her she could sue him for divorce as a salve for her pride. But she never had.

Bruce's deep voice brought her back to the present.

"Even this heat is a relief after all that noise," Bruce sighed, staring out at the view, mentally noting each new skyscraper slicing the horizon.

"Music...not noise," Diana amended gently, a slight smile curving her lips.

"What passes for music to your illiterate generation. Damn, it makes me feel old just to listen to it and to watch those kids jump around hour after hour."

"Bruce, you're not old...."

"Thank you, my dear." He smiled disbelievingly. "Flattery will get you everywhere. But to change the subject—do you see that big dark space over there on the other side of fifty-nine, beyond the loop?"

"Yes."

"That's where I'm going to start building the Harroll Twin Towers. We finally got some interim financing that won't absolutely break us. So you won't be seeing much of me at the pool for a while until I get that project off the ground. You can't imagine the mind-boggling details in a deal like that."

"And I thought you were going to slow down...."

"I will someday. You about ready to leave?" Bruce grimaced. "I don't think I can stand much more of this...uh...fun."

"Yes, Bruce, if you are," Diana replied quietly, grateful that Bruce seemed as anxious to leave as she now was.

As he opened the door he shouted above the music, "Say, several of the investors in the Harroll project are in town, and Doug brought them to the party. I'd like for you to meet them."

"Oh, Bruce, I'd rather not."

"Now, you wouldn't cheat an old man out of the fun of impressing his friends with a date as beautiful as you."

"I'm not your date," she denied softly, savoring his friendly admiration in spite of herself.

"You and I know that," he chuckled, "but why should I enlighten my jealous old cronies, who don't have a girl like you around to make them forget their age? I want them to eat their hearts out."

"If you weren't such a dear friend, Bruce, I'd think you had a mean streak," Diana teased, feeling vastly relieved that Ross was nowhere to be seen when she stepped inside. He'd probably made a swift exit minutes after he'd seen her. But, of course, with the Arab decor, she couldn't be sure. Ross could be concealed behind the thick draperies of a tent, or he could be inside one.

"Oh, I do. I definitely do," Bruce freely admitted without even the vaguest twinge of conscience.

There was no point in arguing with Bruce when he was determined to have his way. He loved a practical joke, and she saw that he was set on introducing her and letting his pals draw their own conclusions, knowing all the time what those conclusions would be. They would see her as a beautiful young thing just dying to get her hands on the older man's money—the replica of his second wife.

Bruce drew her forward to a large table lost beneath the heavy draperies of a mock tent in the deepest shadows of the room. When her eyes grew accustomed to the gloom, she noted that most of the men bunched around the tiny round table were obviously affluent older businessmen like Bruce. They smiled at her warmly, welcoming her with delight, as though she were a ray of sunshine on a dim day.

Her own answering smile froze on her lips when she stared in dismay as she recognized Ross, who'd been lounging in a chair at the end of the table until she'd walked up. Her throat had suddenly gone so dry she could scarcely mumble the polite greetings expected of her. She was too keenly aware of Ross and how uncomfortable her presence made him.

His whole body had gone as rigid as hers, though

he sought to conceal his tension and was more successful than she. Casually he reached for his friend's
silver cigarette case and removed a cigarette. He
struck a match. In the golden flare of the light Diana
saw him well for the first time. She watched, fasci-
nated, as he lifted the cigarette to his tightly set lips
and inhaled. Ross seldom smoked—and only when
he was deeply upset. Then, as if he remembered she
would know this, he ground out the cigarette in the
little ashtray near him after having taken only one
drag.

He was every bit as handsome as she remembered.
More so, she thought desperately, devouring him with
her eyes as one would a food one was starved for.
Just seeing him made her tremble. Oh, why, why
hadn't she insisted that Bruce take her home at once?

Every virile feature was so dear to her—the rich
thick blackness of his hair, the familiar wayward lock
falling carelessly across his swarthy forehead no matter how many times he combed it in place, the golden-
brown eyes beneath heavy dark brows, eyes that were
lashed with the longest and densest of curling lashes.

She used to tease him that his eyelashes were too
long to belong to a man. He'd only laughed, demanding to know if she thought they made him look
like a sissy. Then she'd laughed, too, for Ross was
undeniably all-male. And his face, except for the eyelashes that lent a strange beauty to his rugged handsomeness, was the most masculine of faces. He had
a strong jawline which could thrust out stubbornly
when he was determined to have his way, which had

seemed like most of the time when she'd been living
with him, she thought ruefully. His lips were full and
sensual. Why did she allow her gaze to linger on them
for so long? Suddenly she could almost feel their
touch, burning a kiss upon sensitive flesh. Her heart
was suddenly pounding in her throat, and her fingers
clutched Bruce even more tightly than before.

Ross's strong brown hand clenched the crystal
glass in front of him, and lifting it, he downed the
expensive Scotch in a single swallow. His dark brows
rushed together, betraying his anger. He wanted to get
out of the bar, away from this one woman who could
destroy him with a smile, but he was caged by his
own damned pride, which wouldn't allow him to run
in front of her. Hell, hadn't he run for the past three
years? Wasn't it time he stood his ground and showed
her that he'd put her out of his life once and for all?
Still, it angered him to observe her, so serene and
beautiful on the arm of Bruce Dixon, a man whose
business genius he himself deeply admired. It rankled
to see her with a man so much wealthier, so much
more firmly established, than himself. Hell, Bruce
was too damned old for her. That was scarcely rele-
vant, he told himself quickly. He should be glad, he
was glad that she had another man, that she was completely out of his own life. It was obvious that Diana
now had everything she'd always wanted, all the
things she'd blamed him for denying her—a place in
the Houston social whirl, prestige, a successful career
of her own. She'd made her escape from a man she'd
once blamed... Deliberately he cut the thought short

because it could still hurt. Suddenly he was aware of
a bitter taste in his mouth, but he told himself quickly
it was only from that last cigarette and all the liquor
he'd consumed.

He forced himself to stare back at Diana, in spite
of the fact that his head was swimming from having
drunk too much whiskey, for he'd drunk recklessly
ever since he'd seen her half an hour ago. His amber
male gaze ravished her as it swept downward from
the exquisite mouth that was as lustrous as a rose
pearl, lips so moist that he could almost taste their
warm sweetness even after three years, and then down
the slender honey-colored throat. Stripping away the
black gown and seeing instead her full ripe breasts,
his eyes roamed over her possessively as he envi-
sioned her soft rounded belly, the shadowed indentation of her navel, that secret erogenous place he'd
loved to dampen with his lips and tongue until she'd
shuddered deliciously. He knew her so well, her every
whimpering response, for once she'd belong to him
so completely that he'd never imagined that one day
he'd be the one who wanted out. His eyes lingered
on her narrow waist before they fell to her gently
curving hips and thighs. Her skin was smooth—he'd
always loved to touch her—her scent so utterly feminine.

He hadn't had a woman in a long time, he realized
suddenly. Diana seemed all blurred softness and
beauty, and desire flared through him like a hot current. Suddenly the hatred that he wanted to feel was
not nearly so powerful as another emotion that only

she could so easily arouse. Still, he regarded her with deliberate insolence, though he took little pleasure when she flinched and whitened with shame at his bold hot stare.

Ross let his eyes travel slowly up her body until his gaze rested on her pale face. "It's been a long time, Diana," Ross said softly at last, his deep voice vibrating through her.

"Yes, it has," she choked, unable to think of anything else to say. She stood there miserably, aware of the terrible awkwardness between them. His golden eyes pinned her as he continued to stare at her in that frankly male way that was so unnerving. It was as if he couldn't tear his eyes away.

"Diana's my next-door neighbor," Bruce was explaining to the older man next to Ross.

"You swinging bachelors have all the luck," the man replied lightly.

Ross's expression grew even more grim at this remark. Later he would never understand the rush of angry emotion that galvanized him into reacting the way he did. It was all blindly instinctual. Ross stood up, his well-conditioned muscular body towering over even Bruce, making Diana feel very small and feminine in comparison. She was instantly aware of him touching her. His fingers gripped her elbow lightly; their touch sent an electric fever rippling through her so that she trembled slightly.

"Branscomb, I hope you're not going to put the make on Dixon's woman," the man beside Ross tossed out jokingly. "Don't forget, we've all got our money in his deal."

"Dixon's woman?…" The phrase unaccountably grated on Ross's frayed nerves, and he had to force his smile.

Before Ross could reply, Bruce turned and looked at Ross and Diana with real interest. "Branscomb…. Same last name. Are you two related?"

"Distantly," Ross murmured dryly, grateful to Bruce for offering such a plausible and innocuous explanation for his own damnably odd behavior. "I was just going to ask my…er…cousin…to dance. We have a lot to catch up on—for old times' sake."

"Ross," Diana attempted to protest, shocked at his lie. "I really don't think it's smart for us to…"

She felt his steel grip on her arm tighten. "I never was smart where you were concerned, Diana, was I?" Ross countered bitterly, now out of earshot of the others as he propelled her toward the dance floor, the male in him wanting to assert a primitive claim to his rights, even though the logical part of him knew he was behaving in an utterly boorish manner.

When they reached the dance floor, he stared down at her for a long moment, hesitating as his dark golden eyes burned her with their intensity. There was something in his ruthless gaze, some intimate quality, that turned her bones to liquid and made her breaths come in short little rushes.

He shouldn't be doing this! a part of her mind screamed. He should keep his distance! Then there was no more time to think or protest, for she felt her body being swept into the hard circle of his arms as he pressed her closely against himself and turned her slowly in time to the music. Thrilling physical sensations sizzled through her, for being in his arms rekindled old memories of other nights long ago when he'd loved her, when she'd still deserved his love. Hating herself that she had no pride, she let her body go limp as she weakly melted against him.

She could feel the imprint of his hands searing through the gauzy material of her gown to her own flesh as they slowly roamed across her back. Her hand rested against his hard warm chest, and she felt his own heart pounding violently. He wasn't indifferent to her—at least not physically.

She was forcibly aware of every muscled contour of his body, of his arms wrapped around her, of his thighs brushing against hers as he crushed her so close, molding her to him so that she almost felt she was a part of him.

Her arms reached up and circled his neck, while his own locked tightly around her tiny waist, holding her lush curving flesh against himself. It was the way they had always danced—locked together with intimate completeness, as though they were the only man and the only woman in the world. Involuntarily her fingers moved caressingly through his thick black hair.

She had wanted this moment—she knew that now, in spite of all her proud pretenses that she hadn't. For three years she'd avoided him as deliberately as he'd avoided her, returning to her East Texas hometown,

Orange, to visit her parents only when they had assured her that Ross would be away. She'd built up a wall of defenses proclaiming that she no longer needed any man, that love was an emotion that was safely locked away in her past. And now suddenly she knew the truth. She'd been afraid to admit that she'd made a terrible mistake. She'd wanted him and only him, but she hadn't been strong enough to face his rejection. And that wasn't all.

She wanted Ross back—desperately. She wanted to start over, but when she remembered all that she had done to hurt him, she knew she had to stay away from him. For at one time she'd almost destroyed him.

Ross was a good dancer. He moved easily, his great body rhythmically flowing in harmony with the pulsating beat of the music, and he held Diana so tightly, she knew it was useless to resist him.

"Ross," she started hesitantly, breathlessly, scarcely hoping that he might have forgiven her and yet not being able to stop herself from asking. "Why are you doing this? Y-you once said you never wanted to touch me or hold me again."

"Obviously I didn't know then how I'd feel tonight," he muttered sardonically, anger and cynical humor mixing with his desire. "Three years of loneliness, six double Scotches, and that see-through nothing of a dress you're wearing can affect a man in a powerful way," he finished, deliberately cutting her.

She flinched and tried to pull away, but he only strengthened his grip. "If that's all you feel," she pleaded, "let me go.... I—"

"Don't pretend you care how I feel, Diana." Hungrily he wound his hand through her long swaying hair and pulled her closer. "And why should I make it easy on you?" There was savagery in his dark tone. "You're like a witch, a poison in my system I can't get rid of—no matter how I want to. Three years—and I still want you. I still feel…" Abruptly he sliced off the end of his statement, hating himself, she thought, even more than he was determined to hate her.

Suddenly her pride wasn't nearly as important as communicating honestly with him.

"Ross, I'm so sorry…for everything."

"You probably are," he muttered wearily, his anger draining away because he saw the stark pain in her eyes. "But *I'm sorry*'s don't right most wrongs in the grown-up world, do they?" There was a world-weary cynicism in his deep drawl. "I'm not sure you ever learned that. You were always such a child, Diana."

She stared back at him silently. "Not until it was much too late," she said finally with a trace of sadness. "But, Ross, I did grow up. And there's something very important to me that I think I've wanted to tell you for a long time."

"What?"

"That—" suddenly it was terribly difficult to frame the simple sentence "—I—I still love you."

He hesitated, as if he wasn't sure he'd heard her correctly.

She forced herself to go on. "I love you so much."

She strangled back a sob along with all the regrets that threatened to swamp her. "I never realized how much what we had together meant to me."

"Once—I would have given anything to hear you say that again," he said slowly at last and very gently. "After Tami died...if you'd come to me...and said anything...just once...I might... But never mind, none of that matters anymore."

"Yes, it does. Tell me what you were going to say."

"No." He bit out the word.

"Ross, I know I was wrong then. I should never have blamed you for what happened."

"I don't want to talk about it."

"But I've changed. I really have."

"I'm glad," he said in that same cool voice that told her how little he cared. His darkly handsome features masked all his emotions as he tilted his head and looked down at her.

"I do love you...." she whispered gently.

"If that's true," he said indifferently, "then I'm sorry for you."

"Sorry for me?"

"Yes." The old bitterness was back in his voice. "Because I know better than most the hell of loving the wrong person."

"What are you saying?"

"I don't want your love anymore, Diana. I haven't for a very long time."

For the first time she was aware that they had stopped dancing. Ross had maneuvered her into the darkened interior of one of the Arab tents decorating the nightclub. He was holding her even more tightly, his hard hips tightly molded to hers, and she was very aware of his complete masculine arousal. She felt his warm breath against her forehead and caught the faint masculine scent of Scotch mingled with cigarettes.

"What do you want, Ross?" she whispered almost fearfully at last.

"What any man would want under these circumstances from any woman as beautiful as you—this."

In the last instant before his mouth touched hers, the smoldering light in his dark eyes made her feel faint and shivery, awakening all the sleeping yearnings she had worked so hard to suppress. But she couldn't let herself feel like this! A wild desperation coursed through her. She had to stop him! He mustn't! Powerfully muscled arms were wrapped tightly around her, imprisoning her, so that logic should have told her it was useless to struggle.

An illogical panic drove her, and she pushed against him, straining to break away. But she was fragile compared to his tough strength, and her blows fell lightly on his chest. He bent her backward effortlessly, and she felt the flexing of his smooth, hard muscles in his arms and thighs next to her own softer flesh that was pressed against him.

Her resistance only strengthened his own fierce emotion. Ross bent his mouth to hers, ravaging her soft upturned lips. He kissed her again and again, slowly, devouring her resistance. The hands that had been raining tiny blows against his chest fell away.

She felt limp and dizzy. A sweeping tide of tumultuous passion shuddered through her as she clung to him, yielding to the possessive pressure of his mouth claiming hers. Her lips parted provocatively so that his hot warm tongue could enter and explore the warm sweet wetness of her mouth, so that it could mate intimately with hers.

The glory of his embrace overwhelmed her. She'd missed him, every aspect of their relationship, but nothing more than his passionate masculine lovemaking. Because for so long she'd lacked the thrill of such moments, she treasured this bittersweet moment all the more.

The whole world was spinning. Only Ross at the center of her world stood rock-hard, lean and powerful. She clung to him, her arms closing tightly around his back as she pressed her body closely against him. She wanted him to hold her forever, to never let her go.

She was as delicious and wantonly responsive as Ross remembered. His pulse pounded like a violent drum as desire surged through him. His lips moved across her mouth, and he kissed her over and over again with a fierce, savage hunger, until she was damp and hot and breathless from his kisses. He wanted to make her forget everything except himself. Slowly his mouth wandered down her throat, moving beneath the plunging neckline of sheer fabric to nibble and tongue the darkened tautness of her nipple. He ate the warm sensitive flesh with a gentle hunger at first, and then, his own passion consuming him, with a fierce need. Only when her whole body quivered and she was gasping did he stop. Then she felt wretched that his lips were no longer fused to her flesh, and she moaned, a tiny little feminine sound of anguish.

"I want you, Diana, to sleep with me tonight," he muttered hoarsely. "But that's all I want from you—now or ever."

Two

All you want from me?'' Diana questioned. "I don't understand.''

The softly shadowed light in the tent made the pupils of Ross's tawny eyes so large they appeared to be a luminous black. His unrelenting gaze never wavered from her delicately beautiful face.

"I need to prove to myself once and for all that I'm over you, that you're no different from any other attractive woman I might meet in a bar and take home for the night.''

It was a mad, mutually destructive request, and at first she couldn't believe he was serious. He spoke as if it were his habit to pick women up, yet she knew for certain that it wasn't.

"Oh, Ross, no,'' she murmured, struggling with a

bombardment of emotions—hurt, regret and love, the most painful of all. "We mustn't... Not like this...not when you don't really care about me any longer. Why can't we leave everything as it was—in the past?"

"Because I saw you again tonight."

"We can forget."

He laughed, and the sound grated harshly. "I wish it were that easy." He stroked his hand lightly across her velvet-soft shoulder before he quickly drew it away. "Damn you, Diana, for making me want you all over again."

She caught the vibrant note of pain in his deep voice, and she ached for him.

"Ross..."

He placed one finger against the pouting fullness of her lips, shushing her plea for forgiveness.

"Haven't we made enough mistakes, Ross, without this last..."

"If you love me, sleep with me—one last time. Maybe then I'll know if you're completely out of my system," he demanded with utter ruthlessness, little caring that he played on the deepest emotion of her heart.

His words slashed through her with the brutal rupturing impact of a bullet, causing her to wince. He thought of making love to her as an act of exorcising an evil spirit from his soul. She couldn't blame him for feeling the way he did. At least he was honest, she thought ruefully. He wasn't seducing her with false promises. For an instant she could scarcely see him through the brilliance of her unshed tears.

"You owe me that much, Diana," he said slowly. "And you know it."

Perhaps in a way she did, but did he have to demand this ultimate sacrifice? When she stared up into his implacably set features, she realized the hopelessness of her own feelings. She didn't want this to be happening between them—this coming together of their bodies like two strangers when neither of them really wanted it. She wasn't sure she could handle the hurt this time when he left. And yet she was to blame for everything that had gone so terribly wrong between them. Perhaps she did owe him anything he asked. If she could help him in any way…no matter how much it hurt to do so…

"I suppose…in a way…I do," she admitted reluctantly in a tiny shaking voice. She broke off, unable to say anything else.

A long moment of tremulous silence passed between them. Then she felt the strong warmth of his fingers caress her chin, lifting her face so that his lips could easily come down hard on hers once more, branding her with the ruthless fury of his desire until she ached with longing for him.

Both of them felt a fleeting sensation of danger, as though they were being violently drawn into deep emotional waters from which there would be no swimming back. He despised the weakness in himself that made him want her so much that his heart pounded and his breathing was ragged. But she was in his blood, a part of himself. He needed to taste her, to feel the satin texture of her flesh, to catch her delicious scent, if only for one night. He wanted to hold her naked in his arms with every inch of her pressing tightly against himself.

Diana knew she should have protested, she should have struggled, but with a single shudder of exquisite sensation she arched her body so that it fitted more tightly against his lean length, surrendering to a hot primitive force so powerful she could not deny it. Her whole body tingled as his mouth plundered hers in fierce possession. She was totally, elementally aware of him as a man, wanting him, craving him as she never had before. In that moment she would have done anything that he asked.

Swaying in a swirling mist of desire, she felt herself go weak in his arms. He seemed to lift her up in his strong arms and hold her against his powerful body as he burned a trail of kisses downward over her soft throat and shoulders. Their lovemaking seemed to go on and on while each savored the richness of pure physical contact with the other.

Slowly he withdrew his mouth from her shaking lips, though he still clasped her tightly to him. "Then you'll get rid of Dixon and sleep with me tonight?"

"Y-yes," she murmured softly against the warm flesh of his throat.

Her quavering reply was agonized, but he didn't seem to care. In a daze of pain, she was aware of Ross straightening his tie and running a hand through his rumpled black hair. Then he lifted back the folds of the tent and led her back toward the table where Bruce was sitting down, now deeply involved in a business discussion with his investors. Bruce seemed almost relieved when she told him Ross would be seeing her home. Rising, Bruce brushed her cheek with a light good-bye kiss and shook Ross's hand heartily.

Diana was thankful that the elevator she and Ross stepped into was jammed with a rowdy crowd. Thus they descended twenty stories to the parking garage without having to face the difficulty of attempting small talk.

When they reached the underground garage, Ross would have led her to his familiar blue truck, but Diana stopped him, pointing instead in the opposite direction. "Bruce left his car open. Do you mind if I get a package I left in it?"

"Not at all." His deep voice seemed to echo in the vast garage.

She scurried toward Bruce's bright red sports car and unlatched the door. The shopping bag was crinkling in her trembling fingers as she dragged it across the black leather upholstery when she heard Ross's heavy footsteps pause directly behind her.

"I should have known," he murmured, his voice silken and sarcastic.

"What?" She spun to face him, dropping her package in her confusion.

"The car," he said simply, kneeling to retrieve the fallen item from the black asphalt drive.

When he handed her the sack again, she was briefly aware of his hard warm hand closing over her tiny slender one, his touch briefly burning through her.

Then her attention focused on the sleek, thoroughly distinctive, dazzlingly red automobile before her, seeing it for the first time through Ross's eyes.

"Bruce *would* drive a Ferrari," Ross continued matter-of-factly yet with a trace of malice, suddenly remembering her particular predilection for speed and fast cars. "I guess that's what it takes for a man his age to acquire a woman young enough to be his daughter."

When his rough accusation sliced through her, Diana's brows snapped together over eyes that had gone a deep dark shade of metallic blue, and she quivered with fury. If only she could say something that would wipe that smug look from his features.

"Maybe you don't know me as well as you think you do, Ross Branscomb! And if this is your nasty way of prying into my life, of asking whether Bruce and I are lovers, I don't like it. The way I choose to live is my own affair. You gave up any rights to judge me the day you walked out!"

Why didn't she just deny what he accused her of? Because, she thought furiously, it was none of his business!

"Then I have my answer—don't I?" he asked darkly, letting his brilliant gaze devour every curve revealed by her sheer flowing gown. "I hope he doesn't mind sharing."

"Ooooo!" She almost screamed.

His last ugly remark was like a spark plug igniting the fuse of her temper. She reached up and would have slapped his hateful, boldly mocking face had he not seized her wrists and held them tightly, crushing her body against his own so that she could feel every one of his sinewed muscles. She struggled wildly, angrier and more frustrated than ever at being restrained. "We don't sleep together, damn you!" she hurled up at him, tears of humiliation clogging her throat and almost choking off her ability to continue. Between sobs she cried, "There hasn't been anyone except you, you…you odious…wretched… You say you wish you could get me out of your system! Well, I feel the same way. What good is it to want someone who doesn't want you any longer, someone who'll never forget…"

She was aware of his hold gentling, of his arms sliding around her back and cradling her against him.

"Diana," he breathed softly. "I'm sorry. I shouldn't have said what I did. I don't know why I feel driven to go on hurting you. As if we haven't done enough of that in the past."

That was all he said, but it was enough to ease the tension between them. He held her for a long moment, comforting her. Gently he took a handkerchief from his pocket and wiped away her tears of anger.

He led her to his truck. "Would you mind driving," he asked, "since you know Houston better than I and…"

Though he held his liquor well and showed no effects from it, Ross never liked to drive after he'd had a few drinks.

"All right."

She forced herself to drive more slowly and more

carefully than usual, for Ross had always been critical of her driving in the past.

"So what are you doing in Houston, Ross?" she asked much later, after she had braked a little too quickly at a traffic light on Westheimer, throwing Ross slightly forward in his seat. They hadn't spoken since the garage.

Two pieces of metal snapped together ominously as Ross clicked his seat belt together. She noticed that he looked a little pale. "I have investments here— several apartment complexes and a small building I needed to check on," he managed casually.

"Oh." She hesitated. "Are you putting some of your money in the Harroll Towers?"

She was aware of the rugged masculine strength in his carved profile as he turned slightly toward the sound of her voice.

"That's still way out of my league, Diana. In case you haven't forgotten, I'm just a poor boy who's still trying to make good."

There was no sarcasm in his low drawl, and when she searched his dark, unreadable features she detected no bitterness.

"Who's determined to make it completely on his own..." she whispered softly, remembering the difficulties his inflexibility in this area had once caused them.

"That's right."

It was strange, but now she felt admiration for this attitude of his, which she'd once considered his stubborn pride. Since that time she herself had learned the joy of achievement in business. Of course, unlike Ross she'd accepted her father's initial generous offer of capital as well as several other rather large financial transfusions when things had been shaky, loans to be repaid when her business was more successful. How proud she'd been six months ago when she'd begun making monthly installments against her debt even though her father would have been just as happy if she never repaid a penny.

The traffic light changed. She put her foot on the accelerator and didn't let up, and the truck whizzed past a Volkswagen Rabbit that honked loudly. A motorcycle swerved in the nick of time to avoid the truck's path as it raced onto the freeway with the furious energy of a snorting bull charging toward a fluttering red cape. Diana changed lanes, talking as she did so.

"I couldn't understand why you felt that way, Ross, though now I think I do," she said, concentrating more on the thread of her thoughts than on the speeding cars whizzing by on all sides of them. She failed to notice that Ross, who was paying more attention to the road than she was, had gone white when she'd zipped around a bright orange barrel with blinking warning lights, seeming to miss it by inches. "I just wanted to move into town and have a pretty house and a nice car and—"

"And lots of other expensive things I couldn't afford but your father could," he said in a low, controlled voice.

"Mother kept saying she wondered what people

would think about her daughter living way out there in the woods in a tumbledown—''

"Tumbledown!" he lashed, his masculine pride stung, and he ripped his eyes from the road for the first time. "That house was better built than any of those places she kept picking out for us." He caught himself. "Damn! What am I doing? I don't care what Madelaine thought, and neither should you! Diana, you're thirty years old. You didn't have to answer to that woman then, and you don't now. Do me a favor and keep Madelaine out of our conversation tonight."

"All right," she replied meekly as she applied her foot to the accelerator with a vengeance again. She quickly switched lanes to narrowly pass a bus that loomed suddenly like a diesel-breathing ribbed silver monster in Ross's window, close enough to obliterate him if Diana made a single false move.

"Damn it, Diana, it's taken all my willpower not to say anything about your driving, but that bus was too much!" He was uncomfortably aware that he sounded very much like a husband instead of a man who'd picked up a strange woman for the night.

"Was it? Oh, I'm sorry, I-I got so interested in what you were saying that I forgot to drive the way you like me to." She took her foot off the accelerator and slowed the truck to the demure pace of an old lady driving cautiously to Sunday school. Ross sat back in his seat, relaxing. The color came back into his face.

A short while later she resumed the same topic they'd been discussing before. "I just never had been around anyone like you before, Ross. I didn't understand the concept of working for something. I was always given everything I wanted even before I knew I wanted it. I went to private schools where everyone else lived in the same way."

"Instant gratification," he mused absently, most of his attention glued to the road.

"I stayed a child longer than I should have, I suppose. If it hadn't been for our marriage, I might never have changed."

"You certainly didn't want to," he said wryly, smiling for the first time.

"No," she murmured, smiling herself as she remembered how she'd once been. She'd been a spoiled brat, and looking back now, Ross had been infinitely patient with her, though she hadn't thought so at the time. For a fleeting instant she wished she could go back and relive that time—without making the same mistakes. She brushed the thought quickly aside, for there was one thing she had learned: There would be no second chance for her.

Night lights whirred by as Diana drove with increasing speed toward her high-rise apartment. Large traffic signs shot past in a vivid green blur.

"Diana...."

She recognized the edge in his voice and obediently slowed down. When they reached her luxurious building, she almost crept up the drive. Ross sighed in deep relief, sagging against his seat.

"I've never been so glad to get anywhere in one

piece—or so surprised,'' he said. "I thought I was the
one who'd been drinking and shouldn't drive.''

"Then since you've had a few, you're obviously
in no position to judge my driving. Besides, you always exaggerate my faults on the road,'' she replied,
smiling guilelessly. "Why do you always turn into a
coward the minute you hop into a car?''

"That only happens when you're driving," he replied dryly. "This truck isn't paid for, not to mention
the fact that I don't have much enthusiasm when it
comes to letting you splatter us both on a Houston
freeway. I've always wondered why such a demure
perfectionist turns into a reckless speed demon when
she gets behind the wheel. What were you trying to
do out there, blasting past everyone else on the
road?''

"Nothing, Ross. I just don't see any point in creep-
ing along and getting run over.''

"No chance of that! Seriously, Diana, I want you
to slow down, before you kill yourself or someone
else." Uneasily he noted again that he was sounding
more and more like a husband.

She nodded obediently, though she did not look
particularly repentant.

It was an old and very comfortable argument, the
kind that springs between intimates, like marriage
partners who know each other's views on certain sub-
jects so well, they have resolved long ago not to take
them seriously.

The guard, recognizing Diana, waved them through
the front gates, and they passed tennis courts, a jog-

ging track that meandered through a charming wooded area and a large pool. The grounds were lavishly landscaped. One had the feeling of having wandered into a modern garden of paradise, and that the real world was locked safely outside where it belonged, behind the huge wrought-iron gates.

Ross whistled softly as he scanned every detail of their elegant surroundings. "I might have guessed."

"Didn't Adam ever tell you where I live?"

"Adam and I never talk about you."

She pondered the significance behind those words, realizing anew how deeply Ross meant what he'd said when he'd told her three years ago he wanted her completely out of his life.

"This is some layout, Diana. Exactly the kind of place I'd expect you to be living in."

"You make it sound like it's immoral to live well. Daddy bought the condominium as an investment, and I'm renting it."

"How nice—for both of you." There was a taunting element in his deep tone.

How nice... But when he said it, it didn't sound nice and anger flared in her. "Why do you think it's wrong for me to live here?"

He reached across the seat and yanked the keys out of the ignition. "I don't think it's wrong."

"Then what do you think?" she demanded.

Silvery moonlight glinted in the thick softness of her raven hair, and her frosty lipstick glistened, outlining the provocative shape of her mouth. He longed to coil his fingers in the flowing black waves that fell about her smooth shoulders and draw her warm lips against his own. He had to force himself to concentrate on what she was saying because he found her loveliness so distracting.

"Ross, I said 'What do you think?'" She repeated her question, a faint note of exasperation edging her velvety voice.

"That it isn't necessary to live in a place like this to be happy."

"I know that."

"Do you? Then you learned it since we separated. When we were married—in the beginning—we had the ingredients that could have made a successful marriage. We were young and in love, but like most people, we didn't have much money. I didn't think it mattered if we lived in a house in the woods that I built myself or that we could only afford one car, as long as we had each other."

"And I couldn't understand why you wouldn't let Daddy loan us the money for a down payment on a really nice house—in town. But now I see why you felt the way you did."

"There were too many people saying I'd married the boss's daughter for her money. Your own father accused me of that the day we married."

"I don't think he ever really believed that."

"Neither do I. But everyone else did. And you must concede that though Richard thought I was a great executive at the lumber mill, he hardly considered me the kind of man he wanted for a son-in-law."

It had never really been her father who hadn't ap-

proved but Madelaine, her mother. She wore the pants
in the family, and she'd forced him to say something
to Ross in a last-ditch attempt to stop the wedding.
But Diana didn't want to bring up her mother again.

"You know he changed his mind about all that a
long time ago, Ross," she said quietly.

"Well, I would have eventually bought the house
in town you wanted so much. But I wanted to do it
myself, without your father's help. I had invested our
extra cash in Houston real estate before I realized how
desperately you hated our home. Keeping those pro-
jects afloat took everything we had for a couple of
years."

"I didn't hate our home."

"Yes, you did, Diana. I never could understand
why. Even the first time I took you out there…"

She remembered too well. Bright sunshine had
sifted through the trees, dappling the rough-hewn cedar shakes of the gabled roof with gold. She'd caught
her breath at the sheer loveliness of it all, Ross's
charming house, the sparkling bayou behind it, the
dark green forest sweetly scented by pine fragrance
pressing close. But there had been something vaguely
familiar about it all that had given her a curiously lost
feeling. The sensation had been elusive, like a figment
of a half-remembered dream. She hadn't wanted to
stay, but Ross had persuaded her with kisses.

That first sensation of uneasiness had dimmed after
they'd married and she'd moved in. Yet somehow
she'd always wanted to move into town.

"My feelings weren't logical," she said briefly.

"There was nothing wrong with the house, and I should have been happy with it. But I was a child, and because I never adjusted to living out there, I didn't attempt to understand how much it meant to you."

She was aware of his dark gaze wandering over her face, an oddly intent expression flashing across his swarthy features.

She understood now. Not only had he been rightfully proud of their home, he'd wanted to become financially established before he attempted to afford a luxurious life-style. It had been doubly important to Ross to make a lot of money because she'd come from such a wealthy family. She knew now that with his simple tastes, he didn't have much need for the luxuries in life that she'd thought she couldn't live without, even for a few years. She'd always had everything money could buy, so it had taken her a while to learn that one could do without a great many things and never miss them, if one had the love of a man like Ross. That was another lesson she'd learned too late.

His deep voice caressed her suggestively in the darkness. "Why don't we continue this conversation upstairs?"

Her blood flowed as hot as fire at his invitation, scalding her cheeks with bright color. He sat beside her, still as a statue, as though he were carved of rock, yet she knew that he was all too vitally male and alive. There was something dangerous in his manner that evoked a primitive response in her own senses.

She drew herself up rigidly, squaring her shoulders with resignation to make good the bargain she'd made.

His harsh laughter suddenly filled the cab of the truck. "A prisoner facing the firing squad couldn't look any more reluctant than you do," he stated, perceiving her feelings with uncanny accuracy.

"That's exactly how I feel."

"No, love," he murmured softly, reaching for her. "It's how you want to feel." Her pulse accelerated alarmingly as he drew her to him. "But you can't, Diana, no matter how hard you try."

"Ross..." she whimpered faintly in protest, but his tousled black head descended to her waist and he blew a warm wet kiss through the filmy fabric of her gown to the sensitive flesh of her navel, causing delicious shivers to race through her. She struggled against the intoxicating sensation that flooded her, trying to twist away from the erotic heat of his mouth, but he wouldn't let her move an inch. He kissed her again and again through her sheer gown until she was breathless. Weakly she pressed his head more tightly against herself.

He lifted his head; his golden eyes stared deeply into hers with such intensity that she was sure he saw every secret of her soul. "You want to go upstairs as much as I do. Don't you?" he queried softly.

"I..."

She was very aware of his hands moving lightly over her, touching her intimately.

"Don't you?" his deep voice persisted.

She felt hot and shivery and thoroughly aroused.

"Y-yes...." she murmured at last, stumbling over the admission.

But what was the use of denying the truth? A deep sensuality had been between them for years, even before they fell in love. It was between them still, in spite of all the heartache and tragedy that had driven them apart.

Suddenly she knew that she desperately wanted Ross to make love to her again, no matter what his reasons. She knew that only in his arms, in the swirling rapture of belonging to him once again, could she find at least a momentary solace for all she'd lost.

Three

Ice cubes clinked against crystal. Diana's movements were quick and jerky as she splashed Scotch into one glass and Fresca into another.

"Easy on the Scotch, Diana," Ross said, flashing her a smile that she didn't see. She was too busy nervously wrapping a paper napkin around his glass.

He knew her mood. She'd been busy ever since they'd come up. She would keep doing little chores until he made her stop. If she could have dragged out a dust cloth or switched on the vacuum, she would have but those activities would have been too obvious. Instead she began rearranging several glasses on the shelves.

He smiled again, this time to himself, and looked away. He'd give her a few minutes to adjust to his

presence in her home. While he waited he let his eyes
roam over the luxurious penthouse. He was curious
about it, about where she lived and about how she
lived, though he didn't want to be. He'd planned this
as an impersonal sexual episode that would erase forever a woman who had cost him far too much.

Even for Madelaine the place was lavish, not his
sort of place at all, but Diana had done wonders with
it. It was charming, comfortable instead of intimidat-
ing. Even though it was picture-perfect, the ambience
was such that the bare-feet-on-the-coffee-table crowd
would have been as welcome as a black-tie dinner
party.

Painted white with soft blue couches and throw
rugs, Diana's penthouse had a fresh open-air quality.
A low potted palm stood in one corner in a giant
Mexican pot. Super-large windows and doors opened
onto balconies that ran along three sides of the building, overlooking Houston's dazzling skyline. White-
walls soared upward beneath giant white beams to a
hexagonal cupola, a boldly dramatic architectural feature that during daylight drenched the golden oak
floors beneath with sunshine.

The house was kept perfectly, too perfectly to suit
Ross, but then that was Diana. The floors gleamed
with fresh wax; the white mantel above the fireplace
was glossily dustless. No stray magazines littered the
coffee table. Every item in the room had been carefully selected and artistically arranged. With a glance
he took in the neatly shelved leather-bound books
trimmed in gold, treasured blue porcelains and the

splash of vivid yellow and pink potted tulips on a low table. Diana's mania for perfection in her housekeeping could be directly attributed to Madelaine and the intense dread she had of her mother's criticism. A vague feeling of irritation rippled through Ross before he forced his train of thought away from his dominating mother-in-law.

Ross's eyes wandered to the sculptured staircase that led up from the living area to the bedrooms. He wondered about her bedroom, what it was like. She'd sounded furiously sincere when she'd said there hadn't been anyone in her life except him. Roughly he tried to push the thought from his mind, for it kept recurring and made him strangely uncomfortable— not that he wanted there to be other men in her life. For he didn't. There! That was it—the thing that nagged him and made him so uncomfortable. He still felt damnably possessive where she was concerned.

If he was smart he'd turn on his heel and walk out the door. Nothing was stopping him, least of all Diana. He heard the clatter of glasses on the shelves and knew that she was at a loss to know what to do with herself. But he never even looked toward the door. Instead he strode more deeply into the room, brushing against a clump of soft ferns in a large brass pot, and shrugged out of his jacket, slinging it carelessly over the arm of a stuffed chair. Hell, he'd summed it up earlier in the evening when he'd led Diana onto the dance floor. When had he ever been smart where she was concerned?

Ross turned back to Diana just as she was sweeping

back a cloud of dark hair that had fallen across her
cheek. She tossed her head. The gesture was somehow one of exquisite feminine grace. His gaze lingered on the pale curve of her neck. She was frowning
slightly as she fingered the last glass on the shelf. No
doubt she was wondering what she could do next to
distract herself from her guest and what his presence
meant. Ross thought she looked terribly lovely, fragile and vulnerable. Suddenly it bothered him that he
was the cause for her distress. Then he caught himself. Why should he care how she felt? Deliberately
he squashed the protective feeling that rose up in him.

"Your home is very beautiful," he said smoothly,
moving toward her. "It suits you somehow. The
wide-open spaces, the views.... I remember your saying once that living in the forest gave you a shut-in
feeling."

"Thank you, Ross," she said simply, ignoring his
remark about the forest, glad too that he'd said nothing further about how opulently she lived.

As he reached for his drink she felt his warm fingers brush her own lightly, and she drew back
quickly, starting at her volatile physical awareness of
him. He had only to touch her, and she knew she still
belonged to him as completely as she had on their
wedding night. A sharp pang stabbed her, for Ross
no longer belonged to her.

"I do enjoy the views when I'm home," she said,
searching for a safe topic, "especially on clear days
when there isn't much smog. Texas has such beautiful

blue-blue skies, great big pillowy thunderheads. And then when there's a full moon, it's especially lovely.''

"I know all about Texas skies," he stated matter-of-factly, his comment causing her to realize how pointless what she'd said must have sounded.

"Would you like some music?" she said a little too brightly, not meeting his eyes as she started to glide past him on her way toward the stereo.

"That would be nice," he answered, his tawny gaze lingering on the swaying motion of her hips as she moved away from him. She had the tiniest waist; he could almost span it with his hands. "But why don't you...get into something..." He stopped himself abruptly, realizing uneasily once again how easy it was to fall into old habits with her.

"More comfortable?..." she finished the ancient cliché that had been a sexual ritual between them. When they had been living together, it had always been the way he asked her to make love. Her voice sounded oddly mechanical, not like hers at all, and as her eyes met his for the first time she noticed how brightly flushed she was.

"Exactly. I'll choose the music," he said pleasantly, his voice deliberately unemotional, the tone he might use to discuss the weather, "while you undress."

How could he be so casual, her mind stormed, when she herself felt like she was falling to pieces. Every word, every glance in his direction was torture. She would have left the room, but he caught her by the hand and pulled her to him, turning her in his arms so that her back was to him.

"Here, let me help you," he murmured, seeming not to notice that she stood as still and numb as a wooden statue.

Deftly he undid the zipper of her black evening gown, and then he unhooked her filmy bra. His warm hard hands slid inside her dress, caressing her soft flesh, sliding over her body with expert familiarity, knowing just how to touch her so that every sense was inflamed. Her numbness was gone, and she shivered, awash in delicious sensations. He pulled her hard against himself, so that she felt the inflexible contours of his muscular thighs against her hips, his masculine shape telling her how completely she aroused him. Then he buried his lips in her hair, kissing the sensitive place beneath her earlobe until she melted against him.

"Go on upstairs," he said at last, releasing her.

"Ross..." She turned, gazing up into his dark face, hoping to see some sign of tenderness there, but saw only desire. She took his large hand in her smaller one, and bringing it to her lips, blew a gentle, sweet kiss between his fingers. "I won't be long," she whispered up to him, smiling, her gaze smoldering.

Her face was that of an angel, yet there was something wild and wanton in her expression that provoked all his erotic fantasies. This startling contrast was the essence of her attraction for him. He stared down at her, bemused, and reached for her again, but she was already running lightly away from him.

He watched her graceful retreat up the stairs, her wispy gown flowing around her lithe curves, her waves of dark hair falling loosely about her shoulders. He frowned. Even after living with her for five years, she was still an enigma to him. She was beautiful and gently reserved on the surface, always dressing with meticulous care, keeping her house so perfect, it was impossible to imagine her living in it. Yet underneath this placid facade he alone knew that she was passionately restless, wild, even perhaps afraid. She sought control because there was an uncontrolled element in her nature. He thought of her recklessness when she drove, her total abandon when he'd made love to her. He wondered suddenly if he would ever figure her out.

Ross set a stack of records on the turntable and switched on the stereo. The room was immediately enveloped in sensuous sound. He moved about the room observing everything. There was a recent picture on the mantel of Adam and Diana at the beach, and he went over to it and studied it, wondering who had taken the picture. Dixon, no doubt. Ross frowned deeply. The photo was excellent in quality, the exposure perfect, the focus exact, obviously the product of a very expensive camera and expert photographer. But the thing that caught his attention and held it was that Diana wasn't wearing much beneath that lacy coverup as the surf splashed over her ankles. She was laughing down at Adam as though she were thoroughly enjoying herself. Ross could almost hear her velvet, lighthearted sound. He realized that he hadn't heard her laugh like that in a long time, and suddenly he was reminded of other times when she had laughed, when she had been happy with him and of how much he had once loved her.

He shouldn't have come! He'd known that all along, of course. He set the picture back down, resolving to go before she returned. He was reaching for his jacket when Diana softly called down to him.

"Don't go, Ross. Not just yet."

Her voice was whispery, deliberately seductive. He glanced upward toward the sound of it. She was standing on the landing at the top of the stairs in the glow cast by a slanting ray of light from her bedroom lamp.

He caught his breath—momentarily dazzled—then he expelled it. "Good grief!"

She looked uncertain for a moment when he said that, as though she wasn't sure whether or not he was pleased, and then she recovered herself. She was wearing a dressing gown of white satin. A wreath of ostrich feathers enveloped the slender column of her throat like a soft cloud and splashed like the foamy ripple of a wave down the front of her gown to the floor. Her hands and wrists glittered, and he saw the same white gems dangling from her ears. Diamonds. She was aflame with their fire. The shimmering gown clung to her every curve, and he could see her soft body beneath the sheer fabric.

He drew another deep, shocked breath, remembering the time in New Orleans when he'd first seen her in that gown, a present that he'd given her himself after she'd seen it in a boutique window near Bourbon Street and had asked playfully what kind of woman wore something like that. That night in their hotel room she'd romped around in that gown, trying to act the part of the sultry temptress. They'd been so much in love then, so happy. He didn't want to remember, but he couldn't stop himself.

Tonight she would have looked the temptress, had her expression not been that of an ingenue. But the seductive sophistication of the gown merely made her look terribly young and vulnerable.

She descended the stairs slowly, the slashed opening at the front of the gown falling apart to reveal the shapely curve of her legs as she walked. Her every movement was deliberately sexy, wantonly provocative, and the jacket he was holding slipped through his fingers to the floor.

"What the hell are you trying to prove?" he asked hoarsely, going toward her, wishing that it was anger he felt instead of desire. He halted abruptly, catching the whiff of a strong exotic fragrance.

"I thought you wanted me to act like I was a sexy stranger you picked up for the night," she said breezily with mock boldness. "I'm only trying to please you."

The little minx! "What kind of perfume did you take a bath in?" he demanded, moving farther from her to escape the almost intoxicating scent.

"Oh, that," she purred, flashing him a bright, seemingly innocent smile. "I suppose I did dab on a little too much...." Actually she'd been so nervous she'd clumsily spilled it.

"A little? That's an understatement if I ever heard one. I feel like I've fallen head-first into a vat of perfume."

"Well, if you don't like it, I can go shower."

"Never mind, I think I'm getting used to it."

She moved away from him toward the blue area rug beneath the couches, her cloying scent following her. For the first time he noticed that in one hand she held the edge of a thick white turkish bathtowel, and that it trailed behind her like a furry train as she walked away from him.

Only Diana would dress so provocatively and carry a towel at the same time. He was suddenly so deeply amused by her incongruous charade, he almost laughed. He should have guessed. Diana had always insisted on lying on a towel when they'd made love on the floor. He watched as she tossed the towel onto the carpet, bending over, the swelling curve of her luscious hips in full view as she carefully smoothed it out.

"You should have left the towel upstairs, and you would have looked more the part of a modern siren," he commented dryly. "Wantons shouldn't worry about being tidy when they make love."

"That's what makes me different," she said, smiling a slow, secret smile, not in the least perturbed as she languidly lay down, her white gown sliding up to her thighs. "I'm a tidy wanton."

Ross hesitated for only an instant before he strode

toward her and knelt down beside her. The music swirled around them both. His eyes met hers for a long moment, and he knew that he would never forget the expression on her beautiful face. Then she reached up with trembling fingers and loosened his tie.

A fine tremor shuddered through her whole body, and the knot proved too tricky for her clumsy fingers.

"Here, let me help you," he said huskily, impatiently.

"No, Ross," she murmured, gently brushing his hands aside. "I want to undress you. It's been so long." There was a strange wistfulness in her voice that caught at his heart. "There...."

Slowly she pulled his tie from his collar and laid it neatly on the nearby coffee table, beside the profusion of tulips. Her fingers then ran lightly down the front of his shirt, unbuttoning it to reveal a strip of bronzed flesh. For an instant she knelt and placed her cheek against his warm chest, nestling against the thick mat of bristly black hairs that covered it. It was an affectionate more than a sexual gesture, something she'd done every night when they'd been married.

"Oh, Ross, why did you have to come back into my life?" she murmured, all of her boldness evaporating as she cuddled against him.

She still lay with her cheek upon the hard warmth of his chest, her fingers lightly caressing the flatness of his stomach. He moved his hand through the flowing masses of her hair, gently stroking her.

"It was bound to happen, Diana, our paths crossing. I'm surprised it hasn't happened before."

"I suppose you're right."

"It's only that we've both been so determined to avoid each other."

"Yes," she whispered. "I guess we were afraid of getting involved...which is exactly what's happened."

"I'd hardly call sleeping with each other one night *involved*," Ross muttered. "A sexual encounter doesn't have to be more than satisfying an appetite."

Or it could involve the entirety of one's soul, she thought. "Like eating a hamburger when you're hungry," she offered dismally.

"Exactly."

A knot of pain twisted her insides, but she managed a brave smile. "I don't like thinking of myself as a hamburger to be munched and quickly digested."

"That was your smile, not mine. But I think we've exhausted this subject. You were going to undress me," he said pleasantly, languidly stretching his taut muscles in anticipation.

"I...I..." She lifted her head, her flowing hair sweeping his chest like a soft brush as she stared at his masculine features. His eyes were closed, his long thick lashes curling against his dark skin. He was waiting for her to give him pleasure after telling her that she meant nothing to him. Her fumbling fingers pushed at the opening of his shirt, and then she stopped, frozen. "I...I...can't..." she said at last. She wanted to. She really did, but she just couldn't. Not like this. "I thought I could, but I can't. I'm sorry, Ross."

His golden eyes snapped open, and he regarded her in frustrated surprise. She started to rise, but he caught her wrists and pulled her back down, holding her tightly.

"Not so fast!" he growled, beginning to grow genuinely annoyed as he sensed how completely her mood had altered. "You little tease."

"Let me go!" she begged. "Please...don't make me..."

"Don't make you! Who's seducing who? You made a promise at the nightclub, remember. You just walked down those stairs dressed like a 1930s film queen vamp in that see-through gown you wore the night I made love to you until dawn. Then you led me over here promising to undress me, with that femme-fatale look in your eye. I was lying here complacently waiting to be ravished by a—" his dark glance swept downward over shining satin and bunched white feathers as he searched for the right words to describe such a fantastic vision "—an exotic...sweet-smelling bird of paradise." There was the lingering trace of a smile in his voice. "What changed your mind, if you don't mind my asking? Not that inane conversation about sex being like eating a hamburger!"

"No...I..." She couldn't tell him that she'd worn the gown he'd given her hoping that he might soften his attitude just a little.

"We made a bargain tonight—you and I—and I intend to see that we keep it."

He grabbed her shoulders and pulled her back

down so that her slender body was arousingly aligned with his. She struggled wildly, her every desperate movement only heightening his desire, only increasing his determination to have her. Her satin dressing gown fell open, revealing the soft allure of her feminine body to his golden masculine gaze.

Only when she was breathless did she stop fighting him and lie still, her heart pounding fiercely, her breath coming in rasps. Her gown having fallen off her shoulders, she was crushed tightly against his chest, her bare breasts flattened against his hard muscular contours. He held her so tightly that the tiny buttons of his shirt cut into her sensitive skin.

"Are you going to rape me?" she asked helplessly.

"Rape?" He loosened his grip. At first he laughed at the sheer ridiculousness of her question. But one look into her large luminous eyes told him that she was serious. "That won't be necessary," he replied tersely.

"Then what?"

Already his hands on her body had gentled and started to roam in intimate exploration. She knew that those same hands moving beneath her satiny gown to caress the soft texture of her flesh could tense at her slightest attempt to evade their touch, so she lay still.

She felt torn in two—one part wanting him with an almost desperate longing, the other, more sensible, part knowing how much she would hurt when he left her. He was using her to satisfy a masculine appetite; he'd been honest enough to admit it. His physical need for her was the only trace of emotion that still remained of the finer feelings he'd once had for her. But what was the use of fighting him when she couldn't even fight herself? And as she stared down into the golden depths of his thickly lashed hooded gaze she knew, as she had known the first moment that she'd seen him tonight, that she was lost. She couldn't escape him, any more than she could deny the traitorous, wild response of her own body.

"You haven't had a man in a long time, Diana," he drawled, his thoughts running along the same track as hers. "Three years—if you're telling the truth." He ran his fingers lightly across the dark button-tips of her breasts, and she shivered uncontrollably, almost moaning when he withdrew his hand. He observed her reaction, a faint look of triumph gleaming in his eyes. "And I think you are—telling the truth." He was suddenly smiling again, his teeth very white against his dark skin. "Do I really have to spell out my method of persuasion?"

Four

There was no reason for Ross to spell out his method of persuasion; the dark smoldering light in his eyes left her in no doubt as to what it would be. He who knew her body better than she knew herself, would seduce her effortlessly with his ardent caresses and his hungry kisses. Even the way he was boldly looking at her now, his lazy hot stare insolently stripping away white satin as he would soon strip away every inhibition, rawly disturbed her.

"Leave me alone, Ross Branscomb," she whispered in a surge of panic. "Go back to that bar and pick up some other woman to use to satisfy your sexual appetite," she cried, hoping to stop him with words because she knew she couldn't stop him physically. "You're no better than an animal. Any woman will do for a man like you." Let him make love to a woman whose soul could not be had in the bargain, her heart inwardly cried.

"That's where you're wrong," he murmured with infuriating blandness. "There's only one black-haired witch I need to get out of my system—permanently—and that's you, my sweet."

"You ... you ... rotten ... bullying ... beast." She choked on the only suitable expletive that readily came to her mind. "You hate me and yet you..."

"You can call me all the names you like, Diana," he returned calmly. "I probably deserve a few of them, but I'm not leaving—that is, not until I've had my fill of you."

His arms curved punishingly about her shoulders as he pushed her onto her back on top of the rectangular strip of towel covering the soft carpet.

"Ross," she cried as he followed her down. "Don't do this... It'll cost us both too much!"

"Shut up, "Diana!" He ground out the order through a stubbornly clenched jaw. "You're probably right, but I'm past caring right now."

Her startled cry of retaliation was smothered by hard lips violently clamping down on hers. His male mouth savagely ravaged the swollen sweetness of her lips as his hands roamed her body, caressing secret, moist, feminine places, until her whole body seemed to ripple wantonly with desire. She fought against the tide of passion that was beginning to sweep her, but it was like the struggle of a drowning swimmer trying to weakly swim against a raging current. She felt doomed before she even tried.

Ross raised his head to stare deeply into her eyes. His smile was so infuriatingly triumphant that all of her anger was rekindled.

"You're a monster," she hissed. "A brutish bully!"

"Am I?" He smiled, more interested in the provocative lushness of her beauty than in anything she said. "Then I might as well do what any brutish, bullying monster would do under these circumstances and enjoy myself." The rough edge of sarcasm in his harsh words matched the predatory gleam in his dark gaze.

"No...." she murmured haltingly.

The single word of protest was all he allowed her. He lay heavily on top of her, the weight of his chest feeling like a rock wall pinning her down, his superior strength reducing her struggles to pitiful gestures of resistance. Diana had scarcely recovered from his first brutal kiss when her lips were savagely bruised with a second. She strained against him ineffectually, her strength to do so ebbing as strange new emotions swept through her.

Unwillingly, her flesh responded to the angry passion of his. She felt hot, as though she had a jungle fever. Her heart was pounding at a frenzied tempo, racing in time with his.

His hands stroked her warm body, removing her satin gown, caressing her beasts, teasing her nipples so that they swelled in taut erection beneath his expert fingers. Blood seemed to flow hotly in her arteries as his hands roamed downward to explore the silken inner flesh of her thighs.

Then she felt the pressure of his lips against her skin as he skillfully tongued her navel, licking the soft flesh until she moaned with pleasure. She stared down at the thick blackness of his head buried against her stomach. Then his lips moved lower, and a tiny thrilling shock wave swept her as she realized what he was going to do.

As he made love to her with his lips all her will to resist him slowly flowed out of her; his mouth touched all the private places of her body, tasting her as though she were a delicious fruit he had lived too long without. Her every deepest emotion was stirred by the erotic conquest of his lips. She felt warm and wet, aching with a tumultuous need that only he could satisfy. Yet he drew out the moment, kissing her again and again, kneading her softest flesh with his lips as though he were starved for her. She felt wild with the deepest of aching needs. Then suddenly bolts of passion flared through her, brilliant white hot spasms building into a torrent of shuddering passion. His hands gripped her hips. He held her so close that she felt fused to him utterly, the two of them alone in a brilliant haze of golden feelings.

When it was over she lay perfectly still, her mental state one of drifting euphoria. Only vaguely was she aware of the weight of his head on top of her, pressing into her soft, rounded stomach. Her eyelids fluttered languidly open, and she stared upward at the beamed ceiling of her penthouse. For a moment she felt lost, as though she didn't know who she was or where she lay. Then everything came vividly into focus.

She was with Ross, her beloved, who was lost to her.

Her fingers curled into the thick black mat of his hair, as though by touching him she could hold on to the rapture of his love. But the moment of supreme closeness with him was slowly fading, even though she didn't want it to. Hot tears scalded her eyes and began to flow down her cheeks. The sheer exquisite beauty of his physical love for her was shattering. Her chest heaved as she began to sob. It had always been this way with her—an especially intense sexual release was followed by tears. Tears were a way of saying good-bye after having been so close.

When she shut her eyes again, wanting to hold on to this precious moment for as long as she could, he moved, shifting his great body. She felt the tender brush of his lips upon her damp eyelids as he tried to kiss away her tears.

"Don't cry," he murmured softly.

"I—I can't stop myself. I...I..."

"I never like it when you do that. I always feel guilty that somehow I've made you unhappy."

"It's not that." It was so difficult to explain the soft emotion that enveloped her. She clasped her arms around his neck and brought his head down close to hers so that she felt his roughened cheek graze her tear-moistened face. She held on to him tightly for a long moment, trying to find the right words. "I—I'm not unhappy, but when you make love to me and it ends, it's a kind of wonderful torture. It's just that it was so beautiful—what you did. And now it's over.''

"Not quite," he murmured, a masculine chuckle reverberating against her throat. "It's your turn to pleasure me. I'm feeling tortured, but for an entirely different reason."

"I must seem horribly selfish," she whispered, consciously realizing for the first time that he'd given her pleasure while he'd put off his own.

"Just lazy. Come here, woman." He rolled over onto the carpet and eased her down so that she fit tightly on top of him. "Quit luxuriating in your tears and give *me* something to cry about."

She was giggling through her tears as she stared down at his darkly handsome face. "You never cry."

"I'm going to, if you don't get busy."

"Slave driver," she teased.

His every sense was tuned to her and the pleasure the immediate future promised. "Now, where were we," he persisted, "before I had to 'persuade' you...." he smiled, remembering. "Ah yes, you were going to undress me. After that you can do as you please. I'll leave the rest to that very fertile imagination of yours."

As she stared deeply into the golden fire of his beautiful black-lashed eyes, eyes too beautiful to fit the stark masculinity of his rugged features, a plan formed dimly in the corner of her mind. He still wanted her physically in spite of what she'd done in the past, and she realized more acutely than ever be-

fore how wrong she'd once been to weigh so lightly
the treasure of such a man's love. Driven by emotional forces she even now couldn't fully comprehend, she'd blindly wrecked her marriage to the only
man she would ever love. Why? Oh, why had she
done what she did? She didn't know, even now.

Yet he wanted her. She saw his desire as a tiny
gossamer thread holding them together, the last fragile wisp of their former love. Could she take that
thread and strengthen it until it was a mighty bridge
uniting them once again? She didn't know the answer.
She only knew that tonight, this moment, might be
her last chance to show him that no matter how much
she'd hurt him in the past, his future would be bleak
if he couldn't find a way to forgive her. She was
determined to prove to him that she was the only
woman who could suit him so well.

Her lips formed a tremulous half-smile at this
thought. Then she brought her mouth downward in a
deliberately seductive descent to sear his in a wildly
torrid kiss, a kiss through which flowed all of the
passionate longings of her heart and soul. His lips
parted and her tongue moved inside, touching his.

Unaware of her heart's plotting, he lay back, deeply
contented, waiting as her hands slid over him, removing first his shirt, then his slacks and the rest of
his clothes.

Her feminine gaze drifted over him, savoring every
male detail of his body, lingering at the sight of him
so fully aroused. He was as beautifully formed as she
remembered—a broad brown chest, well-toned sculp-

tured muscles tapering to a narrow waist and the flat belly and powerfully built thighs. He had the well-conditioned body of the athlete he was.

He had said she had a fertile imagination. Again she smiled. She would prove to him how right he was. Then she began a slow, tantalizing method of arousal, doing mysterious erotic things that only she, who knew him and every nuance of his sexual nature so well, could do. Within seconds his entire body was attuned to her every delicate movement, his whole nervous system concentrating on what she did, and she revelled in her power over him, in her ability to please this man she so desperately loved.

The crush of her feverish lips moving over his magnificent body inflamed him, as did her other delicate manipulations, until he felt desperate for relief. It was as if he'd never had a woman, as if she were the first after a lifetime of enforced celibacy, so acute was his need. How long was she going to... He groaned, suddenly unable to stand the sensual onslaught any longer, and he pulled her down on top of himself and took her with shattering force.

Their passion was like a raging storm bursting on a desert too long starved for rain, like a geyser erupting and showering parched earth. Greedily they'd thirsted for each other so long that they drank in every drop of emotion—and still they wanted more. Somewhere deep in their hearts they both knew that once would not be enough. Their passions consumed them, carrying them both to new, but this time shared, peaks of fulfillment.

They lay back together clinging, their arms locked tightly around each other, their legs intertwined. It was a long, hushed moment, a capsule of shared closeness and completeness, and for a timeless moment Diana knew that Ross had been with her spiritually as well as physically.

Deliberately he forced himself out of the dreamlike trance that bound their two souls together. His arms loosened their hold about her pliant body, and he opened his eyes and looked wonderingly down at her. There was no logical reason why she should be special to him when he willed it to be so different, and yet in that moment he knew that she still was. Tonight had not erased her from his life; it had merely underscored how deeply he still wanted her.

All the anguish she'd caused him was pushed to the recesses of his mind, banished by her own extravagant beauty and his male vulnerability to it. Vaguely he sensed that the anger and the bitterness he felt for her would come back, but for now all he could feel was the sated relief and tranquil exhaustion of a man who'd known complete release for the first time in three years. She could give him that, and there was no other woman who could.

His lingering gaze drifted over her, and he wondered how long it would be before they would do it again. Already her luscious body evoked in him the first familiar warming sensations that would readily lead to a new blaze of desire.

Her creamy skin was faintly flushed, her raven hair tumbled in wild profusion. She was exquisitely beautiful, her expression drowsily voluptuous, yielding, her smile one of gentle contentment. Yet he knew when he wanted her again, she would be willing.

He made love to her again and again that night, each time hoping that he would find in physical release a new freedom from her. But each time he felt more tightly bound than ever before. She was a witch who possessed him, a siren who held him with the lure of her sensual responsiveness when her soft body melded with his in the age-old sensual dance of the flesh.

Golden sunlight spilled through tall windows and splashed Ross's face with brilliance. His head pounded. Indeed, his whole body ached. Groggily he grabbed a ruffled pillow and covered his eyes, but with this single movement the entire bed began to move. He sprang bolt upright instantly, and then he lay back relaxing, this time enjoying the soothing swaying motion of the bed.

The bed, a tumble of thick fluffy coverlets and embroidered linens, hung from the ceiling, each corner suspended by a thick brass chain. Vaguely he remembered making love to Diana long into the night while the bed swung back and forth as they did so. It had been a novel and delightful experience.

Diamonds like fragments from a broken mirror glittered from the thick blue carpet. He was smiling as he remembered her in them. Wearing nothing but those gleaming jewels, she'd lain in the bed laughing up at him.

"You must have thought me a silly little fool playing dress up," she'd giggled, "when I came down those stairs."

"I didn't think that at all," he'd returned gallantly.

"I only wanted to look sexy and wild."

"Then you succeeded," he'd replied, aware of his own rising passion, thinking how lovely she was with her eyes flashing as brilliantly as the gems that adorned her body. Not long afterward the bed had begun swinging back and forth as their bodies rocked gently together.

He pushed the pleasant memory from his mind. Idly he wondered if his bedroom ceiling was high enough for such a contraption. He would have to ask Diana.

Diana.... He groped for her warm lush body and discovered that she was gone. The only trace of the rich shimmering spray of raven satin that had recently covered the pillow beside his was a faint indentation, still warm when he touched it.

Maybe it was for the best, he mused, rubbing the painful place at his temples. He would have undoubtedly given in to the temptation the sight and feel of her naked body would have stirred in his loins. He lay back, aware of a deep fatigue, but sleep eluded him as a loud motor was switched on. Downstairs a vacuum was zooming across gleaming oak floors and area carpets, all unwanted traces of their lovemaking being swept neatly away.

He rose from the bed in an unusually good humor despite his headache and sore muscles. He pictured the driving force behind that roaring machine. Her delicate beauty came vividly into his mind. His "tidy Wanton..." He chuckled. He was laughing still while he showered and dressed.

She was in the kitchen when he came down the stairs. The living room was spotless, as Ross expected it to be, the vacuum nowhere to be seen. The only sound was that of the incessant hum of the air-conditioning and the faint, distant whir of a washing machine locked safely away in a utility room. No doubt she was washing towels.

The rich aroma of brewing coffee filled the air. Uneasily Ross realized how pleasant waking up in a house that contained a woman could be—so different from waking up alone and having to get Adam off to school by himself.

"Good morning," he called briskly from the doorway.

A knife slipped through Diana's trembling fingers onto an immaculate Corian counter top where she had been chopping vegetables to put into an omelet.

Briefly he noted that the kitchen, like the rest of the penthouse, was charming. Blue and white Murano Italian ceramic tiles were arranged under a turn-of-the-century hood Diana must have rescued from a wrecking crew. Broad varnished beams stood out against a white ceiling. All this he saw in an instant, for the force of his concentration was on Diana, who was standing tensely at the other end of the kitchen.

Her full breasts jutted beneath a lacy blond hand-knit sweater. He noted the way the matching slacks tightly molded her most attractive derriere. She would have looked demure had she not worn her hair in that wildly abandoned way, puffily flowing about her shoulders. She could look sexy in anything and at any time of the day, he decided. Just the sight of her and his headache seemed to lessen.

"Good morning," she returned softly, placing a copper-bottomed omelet pan on the burner of the stove without glancing toward him.

Her voice sounded strangely hesitant, uncertain. He noticed that she wouldn't meet his steady gaze. He fought back the almost irresistible urge to go to her and touch her. "Mind if I pour myself a cup of coffee?" he asked coolly, knowing it wasn't going to be easy to walk out on her this second time.

"Not at all...." Her low tone was equally cool.

The kitchen suddenly seemed stifling and small to Diana because Ross had come in. She was all too aware of his every movement as he walked about the kitchen, making himself at home, as first he looked for a coffee cup, then the sugar and last of all the cream. Finally, when he had everything he needed, he folded himself into a chair at the kitchen table and picked up the *Houston Chronicle* and began reading it with the casual air of a man who had nothing more on his mind than waiting for his breakfast.

Her own mind was in turmoil, which made his air of nonchalance all the more maddening. She wanted to scream out the questions that plagued her. "Where do we go from here, Ross? What now?"

But of course she didn't. She watched the omelet

ruffle around the edges before she turned it, and then she served it garnished with a bushy sprig of parsley on a floral china plate atop a quilted blue place mat. She set a glass of freshly squeezed orange juice in front of him.

The meal was perfectly served. A magazine photographer could have stepped into the kitchen and snapped full-color photos of the perfect couple eating the perfect breakfast. Madelaine would have been proud, Ross thought, before he censored all thoughts of his mother-in-law from his mind, a process that had long ago become a mental habit.

"Looks good," was all he said, folding the paper and setting it on the table. As she sank down in the chair opposite him with only a cup of black coffee in her hand, he asked, "Aren't you going to eat anything?"

"I never eat breakfast."

He glanced with concern at her lovely narrow face. "I know, and it's a bad habit—one you should change."

'So you've told me."

"Maybe that's why you're so skinny."

It had always been one of his favorite gibes, one neither of them had ever taken seriously. "Maybe...." This ridiculous conversation was getting on her nerves. Why were they talking about her eating habits when she felt that her whole life hung in the balance? "Last night you didn't act like you thought I was skinny," she retorted at last.

"You're not skinny everywhere," he conceded,

scooping up the last bit of omelet and munching into a flaky homemade biscuit. He'd forgotten how well Diana cooked. "And you carry it well—like a model—if skinniness is something one can carry well." He blotted his grinning lips with the edge of his napkin.

"Damn you!" she snapped at last, her patience breaking.

"Did I say something to offend you?" he asked lightly. "I'm sorry if I did. Surely you must know that if you looked any better I'd be up in that...that swing...dead with exhaustion. I'm getting too old for nights like last night." His gaze caressed her, and suddenly he grinned. "Or maybe I just need more practice."

"That's not what I'm upset about, and you know it," she said irritably, refusing to be diverted by his good mood.

"No, Diana. I don't."

"You know what you're doing, Ross."

"And what's that?" His dark golden eyes observed her with great interest.

"You...you...don't want to talk about last night, or...or..." She couldn't go on.

"Or what?"

"Or...us...."

He stared at her blankly. "Us?" Then his black brows drew together, and a cold fury began to gnaw at him. Did she really think he was fool enough to fall back in with her because he was unlucky enough to be attracted to her?

She saw the change in him but forced herself to go on. "We're not strangers, Ross, and we can't go back and erase everything that's happened—either the good or the bad—including last night."

"Let's get something straight, Diana, now and for the future." He bit out the words with savage violence. "There is no 'us.' All that died the same day Tami did. You deliberately killed it! I told you what I wanted in the bar last night—to sleep with you last night. But that's all!"

She was suddenly as desperately angry as he. "I don't believe you! You're just saying that for the same reason you said it last night—to hurt me! If you really felt that way, you wouldn't look at me the way you do! You wouldn't have made love to me so many times!"

He flinched, whitening as if she'd struck him. But she didn't back down. She meant what she said. True, he had been drinking when he'd seen her last night and astounded her with his crude, hurtful proposition, but even at that time she'd believed he was more deeply involved than he was willing to admit. Now she was sure of it. There had been a depth to their lovemaking that would have been lacking if he didn't feel something for her. Still, after what she'd done, she couldn't blame him for wanting to see their relationship in that light. He couldn't stand the thought that he might actually care for her.

"You have your life—and from the looks of things around here, a damned good one—and I have mine. Let's keep it that way." His voice was carefully cool.

He was determined to mask the strange emotion he was feeling.

Her heart felt a painful rupture, and her expression stiffened. No matter what he felt for her, he didn't want to have anything more to do with her. He was determined to kill whatever remnants of his love remained, and in time he would probably succeed completely. He was well on his way, she thought painfully. But she wouldn't beg; she still had too much pride. "What about Adam?" she asked quietly.

Ross shrugged. "What about him?"

"Our separation hasn't been easy on him."

"I can't help that."

"Ross, I can't believe you feel this way. I know you want to hate me, and you have every right to, but..."

His dark forbidding gaze burned through her. "Are you still such a child that you really think that one night could change everything that's gone wrong between us?"

"No.... But I did hope that it might be a beginning."

"Well, it wasn't."

"Ross...I'm so sorry now for everything. If I could go back..."

Brutally he cut her off. "There's no going back!" He swung his chair back from the table and rose. Suddenly he had to get out of the room, away from her, away from the haunting beauty of a face that was dangerously too dear. Long strides carried him out of the kitchen and into the living room, where he searched in angry frustration for his jacket, which he'd carelessly dropped onto the couch the night before.

He pivoted to face her, injecting all his frustration and anger into his voice. "Where the hell did you hide my jacket?"

"I hung it up," she answered meekly, moving toward the hallway closet.

She lifted his coat from the hanger and handed it to him. He slung it over one arm and moved rapidly toward the door.

"Ross..." She reached for him, but when he left her gentle touch, he pulled away as if burned.

His handsome face was full of pain. "Last night you said you still loved me, Diana, that you'd made a mistake. Don't push me now into saying things to hurt you. I don't want that. I just want to be left alone."

"I understand...."

"Good." He opened the door.

"But there's something I have to tell you. I've been wanting to ever since I saw you."

He turned back to her, frowning in irritation. "What?"

"I want to move back to Orange."

"What?" His expression darkened with anger. The repeated word was like thunder resounding in the vast stillness of the room.

"For a long time I've wanted to open a branch of my decorating business there," she attempted to explain. "I feel like an exile living in Houston. I lived all my life in Orange—until you and I separated. I only left to make it easier for you. Houston's so big and crowded that I feel lost here. My family's there. Adam…''

"Are you crazy? If you move back to Orange, there's no way we could avoid each other.''

"I'm not sure I want to live my whole life trying to avoid the past. What happened, happened. I can't change it now, much as I'd like to. I can only go on.''

"I'm not going to stand here and argue about it when you know how I feel. There's nothing I can do to stop you, but if you're smart, you'll stay out of Orange. That's my territory!''

With that he closed the door, determined to shut her out of his life and out of his heart forever.

Five

Smartly dressed in a navy crepe dress that was accented by a caramel Ultrasuede vest, Diana waltzed briskly across the sidewalk along Westheimer toward Diana's Decors. Diana's office was prestigiously located on the ground floor in one of southwest Houston's newest and most opulent buildings. Six lanes of traffic whizzed by, but she scarcely noticed the whir of tires, the occasional impatient honks, the squeal of brakes, the acrid stench of exhaust fumes or the distant roar of the freeway.

Three minutes ago she'd switched off the air-conditioning of her car, and already her brow was damp with perspiration from the combined humidity and heat. It was late August, the hottest time of the year in Texas. Briefly she reflected that Houston would have been almost uninhabitable were it not for air-conditioning.

Late as usual because of her too-hectic schedule of appointments, Diana threw open the two immaculately gleaming glass doors that led inside her shop, her heels squashing deeply into an Oriental rug as she paused in the foyer beneath an enormous modern brass chandelier to collect her mail. Her long thick hair fell over her shoulders as she bent over, and absentmindedly she swept it aside. As always, she was dressed with studied elegance. There was modesty and refinement in every aspect of her grooming except the wildly gleaming shock of black hair tumbling down her back. It alone reflected that wild undisciplined part of her nature that she took such great pains to conceal.

Dick, her business partner, and a regally attired silver-haired dowager were buried beneath a mountain of wallpaper books. He was clutching a teal shade of carpet in one hand and an aqua bit of fluff in the other. The only sound was the petulant drone of Dick's client. Obviously he'd just explained why some combination she thought she couldn't live without would not work tastefully in her home. Usually when he was thus occupied he merely nodded hello. But today his voice stopped her.

"Oh, Diana, your four o'clock appointment with Mrs. Clement had to be rescheduled. I wrote the new date on your calendar."

"Thank you, Dick."

Feeling relieved, Diana swept past them into the

sanctum of her own lavish office. She sank down into her leather Chesterfield sofa, above which hung a Penne Ann Cross, Diana's favorite Western artist. The painting was of a lovely Indian girl on a windy moon-lit night. Long strands of black hair flew across the canvas, a common theme of that artist.

Oblivious to the decor, Diana propped her feet carelessly up on the horn-and-brass coffee table as she relaxed and pored over her mail. This was the first free hour she'd had in days, and it would give her a chance to play catch-up on her mail, billing and or-dering. But as always when she had any quiet mo-ment, her thoughts drifted to Ross. Maybe that was why she'd been working so hard of late—to avoid quiet moments and painful memories.

A month had passed since the Sunday morning that Ross had deliberately walked out of Diana's life for the second time. Madelaine had driven Adam to Houston for a weekend visit, and for the first time in three years Adam talked of his father to Diana. Deeply angry, Adam had been confused by Ross's recent inexplicable dark moodiness. "Ever since he picked me up at camp he's been acting just like he did when you moved away," Adam had said percep-tively. "Everything I do is wrong."

"I'm sure he has something on his mind that has nothing to do with you, Adam darling. You must be patient."

Adam had snorted. "Patient! That's a laugh. You should've seen me."

She'd run her hand through his thick crop of black

hair and tousled it. "Well, this time when you go back, try for me. Okay?" Then she'd drawn him into her arms and held him close, dreading the moment when he would return and leave her alone again.

Apparently Adam had rebelled on more than one occasion because of rules that had seemed too strict, parental demands that were too harsh, and there had been several unpleasant confrontations. When Madelaine had come to pick Adam up and take him back to Orange, he hadn't wanted to go. He'd clung to Diana, and there had been great unshed tears in his dark eyes. Since that time Adam hadn't called, and Diana had grown increasingly concerned that the problem between father and son might be deepening.

It worried her, and she blamed herself. What had spending the night with Ross accomplished except to make life more difficult for the three of them? She should have refused to even dance with Ross, much less invite him home for the night. Her first instinct—to run at the sight of him—had been the correct one. But another emotion had ruled her—love. That night she'd discovered that the love that she'd believed was dead and cold had been like a fire that had merely burned low. Though the embers had been banked, they were still glowing warmly, ready to burst into flame at the first opportunity.

Ross had not called—not once in the thirty-one days that had passed. At first, when the thrill of their lovemaking had been fresh on her mind, she'd allowed herself to hope. But then, as the days had one by one slowly passed, she'd realized that he never would.

More and more often Diana thought of what she'd said to Ross about opening a branch of Diana's Decors in Orange. It was what she really wanted to do— to go home. Dick thought it was a good idea too. Not only was their Houston business, which catered to the very rich, a viable and successful concern, but he'd confessed that he'd been secretly itching to run their enterprise independently all along. When she'd first trepidatiously mentioned her dream to him, he'd pounced on it with enthusiasm, encouraging her every time the chance to do so arose. She had the capital. There was nothing stopping her, nothing except Ross.

She had told Ross that she didn't want to live the rest of her life trying to escape the past. She had come to terms with it and with herself for what she had done. Perhaps she would have been more noble and admirable if she did sacrifice the rest of her life because of her mistake. But she wasn't noble or admirable. Hadn't she clearly proved the flimsy stuff she was made of three years ago?

A death affects everyone differently, she supposed. One hopes that one will perform with great courage and silent heroism during a time of severe stress. But how does one practice to achieve grace under pressure—if practice is needed? Certainly Diana had never learned such things from Madelaine, whose mania for perfection in everything allowed for no such imperfections as a devastating loss. If one just cleaned one's house and belonged to the right charity organizations and had the right society friends, life would be perfect, she had been taught.

All her life Diana had been haunted by vague fears of disaster. As a child she'd had nightmares that she was lost and all alone in a dark forest, and everyone who was dear to her was gone. Strange unaccountable dreams that made no sense when one considered the outward perfection of her secure life. After all, wasn't she the daughter of the wealthiest and most prominent family in town? Or perhaps the basis for her fears was that she would lose the perfect life that she had. The dreams had ceased long ago, and now that she was older she discounted their significance; nightmares plagued many children.

At any rate, when tragedy had struck she'd been as ill-prepared to deal with it as a confused child. She couldn't have behaved in a more deliberately destructive manner if she'd planned it.

That horrible Saturday morning that had changed her life so completely was etched as vividly in her memory as a Technicolor tableau. She'd been driving much too fast, racing home from an all-morning shopping spree at Parkdale Mall in Beaumont because a nasty-looking storm was brewing and she hadn't wanted to be caught in it. As soon as she'd driven up their drive, she'd sensed something was wrong—no one came out to greet her and see what she'd bought.

She had found them in their backyard behind the house—Adam, Ross, and Tami. Not knowing what to do with himself, Adam looked little and lost. Ross's face was gray with pain as Tami hung limply in his arms. Though she stood silently, Diana went absolutely wild inside, a million unanswered questions bombarding her.

The forest had seemed so dark and threatening, even more so than usual. A scissors of brilliance had cut a zigzag pattern against the black sky. Thunder had been rumbling. Rumbling.... She could still hear that terrible sound.

Slowly, in disbelief, Diana had reached down and touched the pale lifeless face of her child, and in that moment she'd screamed inwardly, knowing instinctively that Tami was already gone. "Why? Ross! Why? What happened?" she'd cried out loud.

"Diana, I don't know. She was playing outside, and I went inside to answer the phone and see about Adam."

"You left her...outside...in the forest?" Diana had made no attempt to disguise the rough accusation in her voice. "I've told you never...never to do that!" Ross had always thought she was excessively overprotective with the children.

"She was only in the backyard. I was gone a minute, and when I came back she was..."

The unspoken word hung in the air as the first raindrops pelted down.

Something inside Diana exploded, and she began screaming hysterically. It was all happening again...

"It's not my fault this time! It's not my fault! You killed her, Ross! You left her alone in the woods! You killed her!"

Ross had stared at her bleakly, his dark face haggard with grief. She'd screamed those horrible words over and over again, unable to stop herself even when he demanded that she do so. Finally, as a last resort, he'd slapped her violently across the face, and she'd quieted. It had seemed at that moment when her cries stopped that every emotion in her had died.

"Go in the house, Diana. You're hysterical." His voice had been so utterly cold, and in a trance she obeyed. Later her doctor had come and administered a sedative.

Madelaine had come over with her maid and had begun cleaning the house, saying that hordes of people would be descending on them soon. Diana had merely stared at them, stupefied. Her child was dead, and all her mother could think of was that her daughter's house wasn't clean enough. Finally her mother had left, promising to bake a casserole. A casserole—as if that could bring Tami back. Perhaps if her mother had taken her in her arms... But strangely, that was a comfort that Diana had never known, not even in her childhood. No, she couldn't blame Madelaine for her own failings.

During those first horrible days Ross and she were totally estranged, and she couldn't turn to him, for he was locked in his own savage pain.

No one had witnessed that scene between herself and Ross after Tami had died, and so in the days immediately following the tragedy and the funeral, everyone had praised Diana for her courage and calm. Ironically, even Madelaine was for once proud of her daughter's exemplary behavior. Numb with shock and a pain for which there was no release, Diana had heard their whispered "She's so strong...."

If they had only known her inward despair, the strange terror and terrible alienation she felt. But the oddest sensation was that she kept thinking that she had been through all this before, that these feelings of loss and betrayal and guilt were familiar. All her life this was the pain she'd been running from. She'd tried to be perfect like her mother. She'd been hoping that if she was, life would be perfect and she would never know such horrible pain again. Again—why did she feel that she'd experienced all this before? In those first awful days she had thought she was going crazy.

For the weeks that followed, Ross was broken with grief, but she never went to him. She never retracted the horrible words she'd hurled at him. She couldn't; she was incapable of reaching out to another human being. Many nights he never came to bed. Then one night she'd found him sobbing in the den, and for the first time he'd reached for her, wanting to hold her close for comfort, seeking her forgiveness, begging her to come to him.

But that terrible strange alienation had wrapped her so that her own pain was so intense she couldn't feel his. "Don't touch me!" she'd hissed coldly, ignoring the stark pain she saw flash for an instant in his eyes before rage at her rejection hardened his expression. Eluding his embrace, she ran hastily back to their bedroom and bolted the door.

He followed her, and when he found the door

locked, he was so crazed with anger that he'd kicked it down. She could still remember the feel of his awesome dark presence in the doorway. She'd cringed in the bed, truly terrified of the violent stranger who was her husband.

He'd ripped the covers from the bed and yanked her bodily from it into his arms. He'd kissed her long and hard, but for the first and only time in their relationship his savage passion had awakened no answering response in her. She'd felt frozen, and she'd known he'd felt her deep coldness. He'd thrown her from him.

"You still think it's my fault Tami died, even after the autopsy report that said it happened because of an aneurysm. Well, don't you?" His dark golden eyes, hollow with pain, bored into her. He seemed to hang on her next words as if his very life were in jeopardy, and she'd stared blankly up at him, her lips quivering, without denying what he accused her of. In that moment she'd tossed away her marriage with the carelessness of a spoiled child who had grown tired of a new toy.

"I can live with a lot of things, Diana, but I can't live with a woman who blames me for the death of my own child! It wasn't my fault!"

She'd only stared at him, unable to feel anything.

"What's happened to you, Diana? I don't know you anymore." He'd begun shaking her, and only when she trembled violently did he stop.

"You can quit looking like you're scared I'll touch you or try to rape you. You're safe enough. Tonight you've finally gotten your message across. There's no chance for us now! Perhaps it's for the best—we've been a strangely matched pair from the first. But I kept thinking that... Never mind what I thought! I've been a fool where you were concerned too long. I'll never touch you or hold you again! It's obvious to me that our marriage ended the day Tami died! It's a custom in our country to bury the dead. I want you out of here in the morning!''

Still she'd only stared at him mutely, not able to think, to feel, to talk. His words whirled around her, and she had to struggle to grasp their meaning. Her marriage was dissolving, and all she could do was feel helplessly lost. Maybe he was right: she was in no position to judge. She felt no love for him; no hatred, either. She felt nothing.

After her first hysterical outburst the day Tami died, she'd locked all her feelings away tightly within herself, for she was afraid to feel.

The next morning she'd packed her things and left, moving home with Madelaine and her father. She never told them the reasons for her separation.

They'd encouraged her to move to Houston and to start a fresh, new life for herself. Madelaine, who had never approved of Ross, was secretly pleased, and she reminded her daughter of all the things she'd had to live without while she'd been married to Ross. Numbly Diana had allowed her parents to persuade her to move. Nothing had mattered to her then. She hadn't felt the loss of Ross as a painful thing; she simply hadn't been capable of feeling anything at all.

She'd merely gone through the motions of being alive.

Madelaine had been elated with the project of finding Diana a suitably prestigious place to live, a grand address that she could boast about to her bridge circle. Diana had let her mother select the most lavish penthouse that she could find. Then her mother had given her *carte blanche* to decorate it according to her tastes. This Diana did mechanically, feeling no pride in her selections or in the charming penthouse that was to be her home.

Months passed before the frozen block of pain in Diana's heart began to thaw, and then one night Madelaine called with terrifying news. Diana could still hear her mother's abnormally shrill voice. "Ross and Adam have been in an accident. Ross's car was totaled, but they're all right."

Bruce had been with her when her mother called, and after Madelaine hung up, Diana had begun to cry great torrents of tears. Though she could never have put her feeling into words, the shock of the accident had made her realize subconsciously that she was still alive, that she still loved, that the death of her beloved Tami had not been the death of everything that mattered to her.

She'd wept for hours, and Bruce had stayed with her, comforting her. After that night Diana had grown stronger every day. Now she felt as though the wound had healed. Of course, there would always be scars, and she had her regrets. Perhaps she would never fully understand why she'd been unable to reach out to Ross, to console him and be consoled by him during that time. She was still baffled by her strange reaction, by her feeling that she'd experienced that peculiar agony before. Still, all that was behind her. She was at peace, as she knew Tami was at peace. She'd had to accept that death inevitably followed life, and that the value of life was not something that could be measured in years. However briefly Tami had lived, her life had been infinitely precious, but now Diana was determined to go on with her own life.

Fingering the edges of a scarlet silk scarf that softly framed the slender beauty of her face, Diana sank into the deep upholstery of the chair beside her desk. Strewn across the glossy oak surface was her insurance file and the forms regarding her automobile insurance. Guiltily she glanced down at them and thought of Ross and all his lectures about her reckless driving. How he would have gloated over this, even though what had happened hadn't really been her fault.

Houston's rapid growth over the past ten years had choked the city's freeway system with drivers, many of them incompetent and aggressive. Over the weekend she'd been going a little too fast on the freeway and had had a minor accident, smashing the front left fender of her baby-pink Cadillac against the guard rail to avoid hitting the little old lady in front of her who had failed to yield right-of-way. Her own car was now in the garage, and Diana was waiting for Ralph, her serviceman, to return her call. Impatiently she glanced down at her watch and realized she couldn't wait much longer because she had an appointment several miles away in less than half an hour. Slinging her purse over her shoulder and rising, she was on her way out the door when the telephone rang.

Lifting the receiver to her ear, she answered brightly, "Hello, Ralph... I'm so glad you called before I left...." She paused suddenly, aware of a strange tension, intuitively conscious that she'd blundered.

"Then I won't keep you." Those deep, cold tones that were faintly mocking could belong to only one man, and Diana sagged weakly against her desk as the husky resonance of Ross's masculine voice vibrated through her. For six weeks she'd longed to hear that voice, but now it was so devoid of warmth or affection that it chilled her. "Diana, this is Ross. Sorry to disappoint you by not being...Ralph."

"I know...who you are," she managed faintly, her pride quelling an admission that she wasn't disappointed, that had his voice held a shred of kindness in it she would have been thrilled. She could scarcely speak. A huge weight seemed to press down upon her, and she clutched the phone tightly to keep from dropping it. Normally she had no trouble functioning like a capable human being, but with Ross on the other end of the line she felt strangely numb and foolish.

Ross broke the awkward silence between them. "I called to tell you that Adam has run away," he said tersely. "He's not with you, is he?"

"What?" she intoned as a terrible fear shivered through her. When she found her voice again, her every word trembled with the intense emotion. Suddenly she was remembering Tami, and all the horror of that tragedy was upon her. A cold queasiness gripped her like a cord wrapped in a tight knot. "He's...not..."

Ross's voice gentled, the mockery vanishing, and she knew he sensed her distress. "I shouldn't have dropped it on you like that," he said. "I have no reason to think he's been kidnapped or hurt. In fact, this whole thing is my fault. I haven't been the easiest person to live with since, er, lately. Adam left a note saying he thought it might cool things down if he got away for a while. Here...let me read it to you." Diana caught the rustling sound of paper. In her mind's eye she saw him unfolding a single sheet of blue-lined notebook paper covered with Adam's fifth-grade scrawl. *"Dad, I just can't take the heat anymore. Everything I do is wrong. I'll be back in a few days when I cool down. Adam."* Ross paused for a long moment, and Diana sensed his acute anguish. "I guess I don't have to tell you I feel rotten about this," he said at last. "If I'd... What the hell! I didn't give the kid half a chance, and now..."

"Where do you think he could have gone?" she asked gently, trying to distract him.

"I was hoping he'd head down to see you. He's been begging to go to Houston, so your place seems like the logical choice."

"You should have let him come," she whispered.

"I see that now," he said. "But at the time I was being too damned stubborn."

"Have you called my parents? Maybe he…"

"They're in Europe. Remember?"

"Yes," she murmured distractedly. In her panic she'd completely forgotten about their vacation. "Oh, Ross, he's so little…to be alone."

"You think I don't know that?"

"I didn't mean…" she began falteringly.

"Neither did I," he apologized. "I've been going around snapping everyone's head off without the slightest provocation. That's why we have this problem."

"Does he have any money?"

"I don't know. He earns money for his chores, and he's probably saved some."

It was the kind of thing a mother would know, not a father.

"Is there anything I can do to help? Do you want me to come to Orange?"

"No." His one abrupt word emphasized the harshness of his voice.

"I could…"

"I said no!" In a softer tone he continued, "I think there's a very good chance he'll wind up in Houston. I'd like you to be there if he does."

Never had Diana felt so cut off from Ross. He wanted to keep her as far from himself as possible. It felt as if the emotional barriers he was erecting between them were tangible forces.

She swallowed her pride and said gently, "You

know I'll do anything for you, Ross. Anything. You only have to ask."

"I know," he said very quietly. She thought that for just a moment she sensed a softening in him. But when he spoke again his words were stilted and cold, freezing the tiny hope that flared in her heart. "But I'm not asking."

For a long time neither of them spoke, and when Ross began, his voice was flat and cool. "Diana, there is something I think I should tell you before I hang up. I don't want to alarm you that Adam's disappearance is of a more serious nature than I've already told you. However, just in case I'm wrong, I hired a professional to start double-checking immediately. The police won't involve themselves in a missing person report for twenty-four hours, and I didn't want to wait that long. By then…anything could have happened." He hesitated, and when she said nothing, he continued. "The man's a private investigator from New Orleans with an excellent reputation in his field. His name's David Procell. He seems to be quite thorough, and so far he's found nothing to indicate foul play or… In fact he thinks Adam will show up on your doorstep in a day or two. He says kids don't know the ropes of getting around by themselves like adults do, and it takes them longer to get places."

"I feel so much better that you did hire someone."

"I'd give anything if David would turn up something concrete and we could find Adam…before tonight." For the first time Ross's voice betrayed his desperate paternal anxiety.

"Ross, I...this isn't all your fault," she began hesitantly, wanting to ease his feelings of guilt over Adam. A warm blush crept into her cheeks as she remembered the night of abandonment when Ross had made love to her. Perhaps subconsciously she wanted to draw his mind to the wondrous passion they had evoked in one another that evening, thereby hoping to remind him of the intensity of the sensual attraction that was still between them, all those feelings that he sought to deny. "It's partly mine, too. I should never have let you sleep with me that night. I should have realized the inevitable consequences of behaving so rashly, of giving in to feelings that...that could be so mutually destructive. If I'd only said no then, but I was a fool! Things haven't been the same since...at least not for me. And I've wondered about you, if your impatience with Adam was a result of... Three weeks ago Adam told me..."

"I don't give a damn what Adam told you three weeks ago!" Ross's low voice sounded strangely hoarse when he angrily interrupted her. "You have nothing to do with the problem between Adam and me, Diana. That's one thing I want you to get very very straight! Six weeks ago I put you out of my life—permanently. Adam is simply going through a rebellious period, and I've been under a lot of pressure at the mill and pushed him when he couldn't take it. I was unfair, but this has nothing to do with you. You and I were finished a long time ago! That night six weeks ago only confirmed it!"

She heard fierce, raw anger in his tone as well as

deep bitterness, but she did not hear that edge of unyielding determination she knew so well.

"No matter what you say, I don't believe you,"
she murmured so softly he could scarcely hear her. A
searing pain welled inside her that he wanted to be
rid of her so desperately, and the most terrible thing
was that she couldn't blame him. She didn't deserve
the love she so urgently longed for, and yet she knew
that no matter what Ross said, he hadn't wiped her
as cleanly from his life as he wanted to.

When he hung up, she held on to the receiver for
a long time, not replacing it in its cradle, clutching it
almost tenderly, as though it were a precious object,
as though by doing so she could maintain, however
briefly, the fragile link that had joined Ross to her.
Suddenly, when she realized what she was doing, she
choked back a tiny moan of anguish and slammed the
phone down with uncharacteristic violence, despising
herself for the weakness that bound her to a man who
no longer wanted her. Wildly she reached toward her
box of tissues to dab at her eyes as she lifted the
receiver again to call her maid and warn her to be on
the lookout for Adam. Then she called the superin-
tendent of her building. After her second call was
completed, Diana realized that she was going to have
to cancel her appointment; she would never be able
to concentrate on drapery swatches and carpet sam-
ples with Adam missing.

When twenty-four hours passed and Ross neither
telephoned nor answered his phone personally when
she called him, Diana was frantic. Someone named

Linda always answered when Diana dialed Ross, and all Linda knew to say was that Adam hadn't returned home.

Adam could be anywhere. He could be in danger, and Diana was growing increasingly anxious. She felt sure that if Adam had intended to come to Houston, he would have already done so.

Late in the afternoon Bruce came by to check on Diana. When she opened the front door and gazed up at his handsome silver head, she smiled wearily. A spicy Italian scent drifted to her nostrils.

"I see there's been no news," he said, stepping into the room and heading toward the kitchen with two boxes tucked under his arm. "I brought supper. Pizza. Your favorite kind—with anchovies."

Anchovies did not sound particularly desirable in her present mood.

"I'm not hungry," she mumbled, realizing that she must sound very unappreciative. "I'm too upset, Bruce, Adam could be…"

Stripping out of an immaculately cut pale jade-colored jacket and draping it over a chair, he interrupted her forcefully. "Don't let your imagination run wild! There's no profit in that!" He smiled kindly toward her. "You're going to eat something, and then you're going to borrow my car and drive to Orange and find out for yourself what's going on. No more waiting by yourself and letting this Linda give you the run-around! It's eating you alive! Maybe Ross and that David will have found him by the time you get there."

"I can't borrow your car! You know what a terrible driver I am!"

"That's Ross's opinion, not mine, and I'm sure he'll be delighted to hear that admission."

"That's one thing he'll never hear!"

"Good! Because he's wrong! He didn't grow up on Houston freeways like I did. You need a little zip just to survive here."

Diana smiled, secretly pleased at the thought of how annoyed Ross would have been at the thought of Bruce actually encouraging her to speed. Zip, as Bruce put it, was the reason her own car was in the garage.

"Sure," Bruce continued, "you could take that rental car you've been rattling around in for the past couple of days, but I don't know what kind of shape it's in, and I'd feel a lot better if you were in my car. I've got my truck. It's the least I could do."

"It's much too much," she said gently. "I should never have called you last night to cry on your shoulder."

Cabinets opened and closed as Bruce moved about her kitchen, getting what he needed. Finally he handed her a plate with a bright red tomato-topped triangle of pizza dotted with anchovies and gently guided her toward the kitchen table. "I'm glad you called. Look, like I told you last night, little boys run away all the time. I must have done so three or four times when I was a kid. I'll bet he's hiding out at a friend's. Maybe a friend smuggled him into his house like Elliot did E.T."

Adam wasn't the sort to run away, she thought dismally, and this would never have happened if she'd behaved responsibly, if she hadn't given in to the desperate yearning of her heart. She shouldn't have slept with Ross in the first place, and in the second, she should have talked to Ross about Adam after Adam had confided in her that weekend.

Bruce continued. "Like I said, he's probably having the time of his life with some pal."

"Surely Ross or that detective he hired would have thought of that," Diana mumbled as she scraped a strong-smelling anchovy aside.

"But you don't know. If you drive to Orange, you can see for yourself. I'll have your calls forwarded to my number, and I'll tell the building supervisor to alert me at once if Adam shows up. Before I'm through every employee on the grounds and in the buildings will be watching for him. I'll carry my beeper so I can be reached day or night, even when I'm on a construction site."

"Bruce, what can I say?" Her violet-blue eyes were luminous with gratitude as she reached for his hand. He really did want to help, and he was the kind of man who knew how.

"Just say yes," he said gently, squeezing her hand in his own roughened one.

"Yes," she murmured, feeling some of her tension drain away as she did so.

His gray eyes flashed with amusement as he stared down at her. "If I were twenty years younger, I'd get down on my hands and knees and propose—this very moment."

As she held his steady gaze, she had the strangest feeling he was telling the truth. Suddenly she felt aglow, as a woman always does, when deeply flattered. "Why?" she murmured softly, seeking to prolong the delicious feeling.

His expression changed subtly, and the magic of the moment was lost. "I've always been attracted to damsels in distress, I suppose. And I've always liked women I could boss around, too," he tossed, lightening the mood between them. "They're a rare breed these days." He grinned broadly. "Your easy yes, was the clincher."

After Bruce left, casually tossing his car keys into the lacquered basket that graced the marble table beside the front door on his way out, Diana began to prepare for her departure. Her every movement was quick and efficient as she moved about the penthouse while she washed dishes, sprinkled water onto her tulips and other plants and packed a small overnight bag in case she decided to stay for a couple of days.

Half an hour later, as she paused at the door ready to leave, her fingertips resting on the light switch, she tried to remember if she'd forgotten anything. She'd called Dick, of course, and he'd agreed to handle the business.

Everything—her penthouse, her suitcase, her person, looked crisply neat. She had that rare quality of artlessly lending loveliness to everything she touched.

The deft twist of a tulip's stem in its vase as she passed by, the snipping of a browned edge of leaf, the fractional adjustment of a picture on the mantel, the skillful draping of a scarf at a neckline. All of these things she did unconsciously, her mere touch like a fairy's magic wand, beautifying all. It was her impeccable taste coupled with this talent on which her successful career was based.

She stood at the door, her supple figure clad in jeans and a lavender silk blouse with a rope of lapis and gold at her throat. Beneath the brilliant chandelier her black hair, tumbling down her back, gleamed from its recent brushing. Because of the lavender silk her eyes seemed almost violet beneath their sable lashes. But she had not been thinking of her luminous beauty nor the charm of her penthouse, but of Adam and Ross.

So, she was going back to Orange to see Ross. It would be the first time in three years that she'd deliberately invaded territory he'd forbidden her, and a spasm of uneasiness shivered through her. She gripped the handles of her leather suitcase more tightly and switched off the light. He did not want her. He'd told her not to come, and she hadn't dared call him to tell him of her plans.

Still, in spite of her apprehension, there was a fragile, lingering hope in the most secret place in her heart. It was like a tiny flame wavering against a dark window pane, a single, lost, glistening thread of light that refused to be snuffed out in spite of the gusts seeping through the cracks between the glasses and swirling around it, a light that blazed with the fierce strength of a lighthouse beam through mists on a stormy night, a warm glowing brilliance that was determined to guide a beloved spouse home once again.

"Oh, Ross, Ross..." She clasped her hands together, offering a silent prayer. "Please...somehow...let me find the way back into your heart! I can't bear it if you can't ever...love me again."

All the anguish in her soul was contained in those three simple words, *love me again*. They seemed to repeat themselves as she locked the door and stumbled across the patterned maroon carpet toward the elevator.

Six

The highway whipped past beneath the powerful red car. Billboards, that looked like giant, colorful cards stacked against the dark green forest, were thickening as Diana neared the outskirts of Orange. She saw the turquoise roof of a Stuckey's against the red-gold sky ahead and the bright twinkle of neon beyond, beckoning her.

Nothing in all this world drives like a Ferrari, Diana determined as she turned off Interstate 10 into curving asphalt that wound like a shiny black ribbon through the tall brooding pine forest. She sank back against plush leather. It was obvious she was born to drive Ferraris and not her sluggish diesel Cadillac, which hadn't responded with the necessary burst of speed when she'd suddenly found herself boxed in on

that clogged Houston freeway. Ah, the fanciful problems of the rich, Ross would have joked in better
days, had he been able to read her mind. He would
have chided her, too, that it was her poor habit of
absentmindedly tailgating at high speeds that was to
blame for her accident and not her car.

This low-slung scarlet car was a joy! At the lightest
tap of her dainty toe on the accelerator, Bruce's sports
car would leap forward with the graceful burst of a
panther's spring. She'd reached the city limits of Orange at least half an hour before she'd expected. Rosy
pinkness dusted the fringes of the sky; the last rays
of the slanting sun gilded the tips of the pine trees.

As she pulled into the drive of Ross's house a powerful nostalgia gripped her. Strangely she felt no uneasiness nor grief, only a quiet sensation of relief that
she'd come home—where she belonged—as she
gazed at the familiar silhouette of the rough-hewn
house nestled beneath the moss-draped trees. She
alighted from the car, her high heels crunching into
the clam-shell drive. She paused, eyeing the house
and its surroundings intently. The faint, tangy smell
of the bayou and swamp vegetation mingled with the
aromatic scent of the pines and the softer, more
sweetly enveloping fragrance of lilies.

Instantly she noted that neither the camellias nor
the azaleas had been clipped in the three years of her
absence. Bending over itself and swaying gracefully
in the slight breeze like giant green feathers, a thick
wall of lush bamboo that she herself had planted now
towered thirty feet on either side of the property, en-

croaching upon the cypress swamp. Everything was overgrown and had an untamed natural beauty that had been lacking when she'd lived there and had carefully manicured the grounds. Then all the leaves had been raked, the pine cones swept tidily away and gathered into plastic bags, the flowers lovingly cared for. She saw that her flower bed was choked with brown ferns. Wild vines grew up one wall of the house, nearly suffocating the passion flowers she'd so meticulously tended.

"Oh, Ross...." She stifled a tiny cry.

The house seemed to beckon her, to cry out that her feminine presence had been sorely missed. She smiled ruefully. If only the man inside...

She had reached the front door. For a long moment she paused on the unswept porch to gather her courage. Even in the gloomy half-light she could see that the bright orange paint she'd selected for the door because it set off the natural ambers and browns of the cedar was beginning to blister and peel.

Strange feelings swamped her. Ross was not a man to neglect what he owned. He'd loved his house and kept it up even before he married her. But now the house exuded a hollowness, as though its owner had lost heart and given up. With an effort, Diana pushed her disturbing thoughts aside and bracely extended her hand and rang the bell.

She heard the muffled sound of a man's heavy tread from within as someone rapidly approached, and she was aware of a vague trembling in her knees. Then Ross swung the door open, and for a long, fierce moment his golden gaze devoured her, sweeping chillingly downward from her lovely, upturned face, down her slender throat to explore her womanly curves before he ripped his gaze away. Savage and bold, his male eyes had stripped her every defense, and she knew that he was aware that she'd come not only because of Adam but because of him.

As she stared up at the lean perfection of his swarthy features, she knew suddenly how much her coming had been because of her desperate need to be with him. Even though his expression was forbidding, she longed to reach out and touch him, to curve her body against his masculine strength. Only his presence could assuage her anxiety over their son; only Ross could give her the emotional sustenance she needed to be happy and fulfilled. But he was determined to cut the ties that bound them.

In spite of the involuntary stiffening of her body, Diana forced a smile. "Ross, I came to…"

His tawny gaze slid indifferently to the fragile vulnerability of her face. "I know why you came." There was a jeering element in his cool tone that brought a crimson tint to her cheeks, for in his golden eyes she saw deliberate sensual appraisal.

She stammered, "N-no, you don't. It's not only because of you. I…was so worried about Adam. I…"

"He's your excuse. Don't lie to me, Diana. You know I would have called you the minute I knew anything. Just as you would have called me if you found Adam." His anger, raw and close to the surface, vibrated in his voice. He made no effort to hide the fact that he deeply resented her presence.

The dense humidity pressed close, and Diana was aware of her palms perspiring, of an inner tension building. Why did she have to be such a coward?

"Ross, it wasn't easy for me to come here, but I had to."

He stood in the doorway, his giant frame unyielding, the chiseled planes of his face harsh, his aura remote. Deliberately he steeled himself against the mute appeal he saw in the anguish of her violet-blue eyes.

"Go home, Diana," he said wearily, pushing the door toward her. "I'll call you..."

As the door began to close, her composure shattered as though it were no more than an eggshell he had crushed beneath his heel. He was shutting her out! Deliberately sending her away! Blindly she reached for the door, and her hand brushed his. As her bare flesh lightly touched the warm bronze of his fingertips, a shock wave rippled through her. Instantly a like sensation was transmitted to him, and he tore his hand from the door to sever their brief contact, but not without giving her the satisfaction of seeing that he was no more immune to her as a woman than she was to him as a man. Since he no longer barred the door, she pushed against it and stepped brazenly inside, terrifyingly conscious of his darkening frown.

His gaze sliced her, cutting her to pieces, but she bravely withstood his anger.

"Ross, please don't send me away! Please..." In

spite of his harsh expression and rigid stance, some inner sense told her that she was wearing away at his resolve to withstand her appeal.

Abruptly, as though he could bear the sight of her no longer, he turned his back to her and strode restlessly across the room like a caged beast.

He jammed his fists into the pockets of his jeans. "Go away, Diana. I don't want you here." His deep voice was explosive, his fury barely leashed. Though he was conscious only of her presence, he refused to look at her. Instead he stared grimly out the floor-to-ceiling windows upon the still brown waters of the bayou and the thick, verdant lushness of water hyacinths massed at the banks. But all he saw was a vision of Diana's dark soft loveliness, of her shimmering eyes.

Rather than obey him she moved more deeply into the shadowed room, stopping a few feet from him. When he turned at last he saw the delicate beauty of her face bathed in the last ray of amber sunlight that sifted through the trees. Her silken blouse, unbuttoned at the throat, clung to the shapely contours of her breasts, outlining their ample curves for his male gaze. Her thick raven hair glinted darkly against her pale throat and paler face, and he was reminded of that first time he'd brought her to his house, of that first night they'd made love in this very room. Why had she come back when just her presence in their home was a torture to him?

How small and feminine and lovely she appeared, even lovelier now than in the past; how sweet was the expression on her slender face. He experienced a sensation of gnawing hunger for her. He wanted to touch her, to hold her.... Desire shot through him like a swift pain, and he knew he had to drive her away at all costs.

Nothing in her expression revealed the shallowness and fleeting transiency of her emotions, he thought bitterly. But even though he knew every flaw in her makeup, and in spite of everything that had happened between them, he was still vulnerable to her appeal. Silently he cursed himself for his weakness.

Tonight he saw a wild panic in her imploring eyes, and he was reminded of her fear that first night when he'd brought her to his home, though it had been engendered for some mysterious reason he'd never understood. She'd never been able to explain her feelings about the house and the forest. Even in the beginning they'd been two people who couldn't communicate. She'd wanted money and possessions, and all he'd wanted was her. When it came down to it, maybe she just couldn't understand the deeper feelings of human beings because she was incapable of experiencing them. He'd tried to reach her and failed. Still, when he saw her now looking so frightened and unsure, it affected him.

Suddenly he was aware of a powerful, masculine need to protect her from hurt and pain. He fought against the feeling, despising himself for having it, deliberately dredging up the past as an armor against her lush beauty and his own need.

"I can't leave you, Ross, to face this alone," she

said at last. "I'm staying, and while I'm here I intend to make myself useful. For starters I'll make us some coffee." Then, throwing him a quivering smile that didn't look nearly so brave as she hoped, she headed toward the kitchen.

Silently he watched her disappear between the umber louvered doors that opened into the kitchen. Her expression had been gentle and loving, her voice soft and sweet. On any other man that sweetness would have worked. But not on him! Not any longer, he thought with fierce determination. He knew her too well!

He began to restlessly pace the den, the deepening shadows accentuating the hard lines of his features. He was so distracted he could scarcely think above the rattle of pots and pans as she rummaged through the very untidy cabinet where he kept them. Suddenly there was a wild clatter as several got away from her and crashed onto the tile floor. He headed toward the kitchen, pausing abruptly in midstride, suppressing with an effort the urge to go in there and seize her and throw her bodily from his house. But, whatever she'd done, she was still his wife and Adam's mother.

Raggedly he raked his hand through his thick black hair. Damn her for coming! Every night that he lived, hers was the face that haunted him. Even when he slept, that same gentle voice accused him in his dreams, "You killed her, Ross.... You killed her...."

How could she have even thought that? As if he could have neglected his own child. Tami... As if he could have ever done anything to hurt Diana, for he'd loved her so, more than any sane man should love a wife. He'd suffered more than losing her than he had from losing his beloved Tami. Her accusation had been a blade in his heart, hacking it to shreds. Diana had walked out on him as if he were nothing, and she'd stayed away without ever looking back. She'd thrown his love away, showing him very clearly how little it had meant to her. Not once had she called; not once had she indicated that she'd felt anything for him until that night six weeks ago when he'd found her in Houston. The minute he'd seen her, he'd hungered for her like a starving man and had hated himself because he had.

She'd stunned him when she'd said she still loved him, and he'd realized she wanted him back, though he hadn't understood why. Perhaps now that she had gotten past her pain over Tami, she really did believe that she loved him. Perhaps she really was sorry for what she had done. Or maybe she had finally discovered that glamour and money were not what she wanted after all. But none of that mattered to Ross any longer. He was through trying to figure her out. Though he wanted her to be happy, he was more determined than ever to go on with his life without this one woman whose loss had almost destroyed him.

Ross vividly remembered the night three years earlier when he'd driven her away. He'd humbled himself before her, begging her for her forgiveness, and she'd rejected him coldly, fleeing from him in terror. He'd wanted comfort in his grief, and she'd treated him as though he were something even less than a human being. He'd been so violently upset that he'd stormed after her to their bedroom. When he'd forced his way into the room, she'd cringed in their bed as if she thought him a monster. Etched in his mind was the paralyzed expression of revulsion on her face, her horror of him. When he'd kissed her, those cool, stiffly compressed lips hadn't felt like living flesh. She'd been so still, unresisting in his arms, and equally unresponsive. He'd realized in that moment what a fool he was to want a woman who no longer wanted him. He'd known then that she believed that he'd killed their child and couldn't love him.

In his hour of deepest need, she'd been the first to turn against him. Still, if she'd come back...then he could have forgiven her. He could have understood that the shock of losing Tami had overwhelmed her. But for her to walk out and stay away three years without ever indicating she cared made it impossible for him to believe her now.

Even in the beginning of their relationship, Diana and he had been at odds on many issues, but always their love had enabled them to find a way to compromise. That night he'd known he had lost her. He'd known that it was best for both of them if they separated. Each day that had passed had widened the emotional gap between them. He had made up his mind he was finished with her, but in spite of his determination to be rid of her, she was still the only woman he wanted. He desired her physically, but he'd learned with painful thoroughness that when he'd really needed her, she hadn't stood by him. The past

three years had been a hellish nightmare of loneliness
and pain he had no intention of repeating by involving
himself with her again. When in God's name was he
going to muster up the guts to divorce her?

The louvered doors squeaked on their hinges, and
Diana gracefully swept into the den carrying a tray
with steaming coffee mugs. It seemed to Ross that the
room was instantly flooded with her breathtaking
beauty as she hesitatingly smiled, her face glowing.
She stared at him wordlessly, scarcely daring to
speak. Then she brushed aside an overflowing ashtray
and several newspaper sections and set the tray down
on the coffee table.

The coffee smelled so good, he could almost taste
it. He hadn't even known he wanted coffee until he'd
smelled hers.

"I made your coffee—just the way you like it,"
she said too brightly. Her blue eyes were brilliant in
her pale face.

For a moment he didn't know what to do. Then he
became aware of her watching him, and he was suddenly conscious of the long silence that had been between them. He'd scarcely spoken to her since she'd
arrived. For a minute he couldn't remember what
she'd said that had triggered his reverie. Then it hit
him with the force of a sledge hammer slamming
against his skull.

"I can't leave you to face this alone, Ross," she'd
said so gently, so softly. The irony of her words tore
through his mind like a million tiny splintering frag-

ments, as painfully sharp as broken glass, and he almost hated her.

"No, I don't want *your* coffee!" he hurled, unleashing his fury, "or anything else from you. You left me three years ago, blaming me for Tami's death, making me face the hell of losing Tami alone. Where were you then—when I needed you?" His own pain made his voice brutal.

His sudden unexpected outburst startled her, and she spilled her coffee, burning her fingers. Shaken and unnerved, she stammered, "Ross, I..."

'You've made a success of your new life. Why aren't you satisfied with that?"

"Because I still love you and Adam."

"Words! You don't even know what they mean!"

"Yes, I do...now.... It kills me that I walked out on you."

"Why should I believe that? How can I believe you're concerned for me now?"

She met the hot contempt of his gaze, and a lump of pain swelled in her throat. "I made a mistake. I don't know why I did what I did. Maybe I'll never know why. For three years I've tried to understand, but all I know now is that I deliberately turned away from you. And yet I want you back more than I can say. I've wanted you back for a long, long time. But until I saw you again...I was afraid to admit...even to myself..."

"When you saw me, you thought I was so hungry for you, you could tie me up in knots all over again," he said bitterly. "Maybe it's more difficult than you thought…being in Houston…alone. In spite of all that fast-paced opulent magnificence, it's easy to get lonely in a crowd, however glittering. And loneliness makes for strange bed partners, doesn't it, my pet?" He laughed humorlessly as he stared down at her hard. His curling sable lashes shadowed his beautiful, masculine eyes, making them seem deep and dark, burning in their intensity. "It even got us—a mismatched pair from the first—back together for one crazy night," he jeered. "You don't belong with me. You never did."

She flinched beneath his taunting gaze, and he continued, "But what a night we had…. You saw to that, didn't you?" His hooded eyes flickered over her, savoring her voluptuous body, recalling with astounding vividness her lush nude form sprawled erotically beneath his, swaying gently against the heat of him because of the motion of that ridiculous swinging bed of hers. An unwelcome rush of heat swept his loins before he tore his gaze away. "You held back nothing. Even when we lived together you never gave yourself to me that completely."

"Maybe…I couldn't," was all she said, feeling wretched.

"Maybe…." he mused. His lips twisted cynically. "Or maybe you were deliberately baiting your line with enough sexual temptation to get me thoroughly hooked again."

She went as colorless as a sheet of paper, and the strength to fight back seemed to drain from her as she sank down upon the couch and buried her face in her hands. Instead of feeling triumphant, he felt like a brutish heel, and he had to turn away to avoid going to her.

"Ross, I never wanted to hurt you," she said quietly, her voice so low and choked he could barely hear it. "It's the last thing I ever wanted."

He pivoted sharply, and when his gaze strayed to the lonely yet proud little figure slumped on his couch, he knew he had to get out of the room at once. Her head was bowed, her raven tresses spilling over her slender, hunched shoulders. "Well, you sure did a hell of a job, sweetheart, for a lady who didn't want to inflict pain," he forced himself to say caustically. With that he strode from the room, pausing at the front door. "But since you're here...and impossible to get rid of it," he continued in the same curt tone, "you might as well make yourself useful. Watch the phone while I work outside, will you?"

She nodded mutely, keeping her face averted so that he couldn't see her glimmering tears. For a long time after the door slammed she sat there trying to get a grip on her whirling emotions. Ross had every right to feel as he did, and she'd known coming here wouldn't be easy. But for once she was as determined about something as he was, and she knew that she had to stay not only because of Adam but to fight for their marriage.

When she finally managed to compose herself, she rose, taking the tray and coffee mugs with her, and returned to the kitchen. Opening the refrigerator, she saw that she could easily make Ross's favorite roast stew from the leftovers and vegetables that she found. Ross had always appreciated her cooking and everything else she'd done for him. It was obvious from the looks of the grounds, the house and the kitchen that Ross needed someone to take care of him.

A tiny smile wavered across her lips as one of Ross's gibes repeated itself in her mind. *Maybe you were deliberately baiting your line with enough sexual temptation to get me thoroughly hooked again.* At the time his barb had hurt her, but now... There were more kinds of bait than sex to tempt a man like Ross, she thought with feminine satisfaction, and she intended to load the hook.

Immediately she began bustling about—cooking, peeling carrots and potatoes, putting a load of wash in the machine, dusting, cleaning, doing all the things she'd have done for Ross if she still lived with him. As she worked with that quiet efficiency that was characteristic of her, she was terribly conscious of the silent phone and of the fact that Ross remained outside, avoiding her even though it grew quite dark.

In less than an hour Formica counter tops gleamed and the surfaces of tables looked scrubbed and polished. Delicious stew simmered over a low flame, its spicy aroma seeping into the room. Carpets had been vacuumed, woodwork wiped clean. She'd switched on more lights and rearranged the clutter in the den so that instead of looking messy, the room looked cozily inviting.

It was a masculine room of vast proportions that contained soaring ceilings, gigantic windows and a stone fireplace. The colors were warm earth-tones, somehow suiting the man who lived in it. When Ross had married her, she'd loved this one room so much that she'd changed nothing; to her, the room was a reflection of Ross.

A vague mustiness clung in the air, the scent of disuse and stale cigarette smoke, and Diana longed instantly for flowers. She loved them for their fragrance as well as their rich, vibrant colors. Flowers and plants could breathe life into even the coldest and most austere rooms. When she'd lived here, she'd filled the house with flowers, and the house seemed empty without them. Suddenly she wondered about her flower garden out back, and quickly she moved across the den to the kitchen door.

Switching on the outside light, she stepped out onto the brick patio to see if anything still bloomed. Immediately she was enveloped by the sweet scent of ginger lilies wafting in the humid night air, and she saw that a few clusters of the white butterfly blossoms on their long stems struggled valiantly amidst a tangle of weeds. Carefully she began clipping the delicate, exotic blooms, burying her nose in their soft petals, thinking their perfume sweeter even than honeysuckle or jasmine.

With a smile she remembered the sunny Saturday afternoon she and Ross had laid the bricks for the patio themselves as well as other afternoons when she had planted flowers. It all seemed a very long time ago. Now weeds crept between the cracks and choked the flower beds.

The phone began to ring, and in an anxious rush she gathered her basket, now brimming with lilies, and hurried back inside, breathlessly grabbing the phone on its second ring.

"Hello..." she answered tremulously.

"Linda?" a man's deep voice queried uncertainly.

"No." Her voice had sharpened with a trace of defiance. "This is...*Mrs.* Branscomb."

She caught the faint sound of a nervous cough on the other end of the line.

"David Procell here," the man said stiffly. "Is Ross around?"

Her heart catapulted into her throat and beat violently at his grim tone. "I'll...I'll get him."

Trying to stave off her sudden panic, she set the phone down on the counter and would have raced toward the front door. But a hand of steel circled her tiny waist, and she was hauled against the powerful length of a man's corded body.

"I'm here," Ross said gently, his hand lingering at her waist, holding her trembling body against his as he lifted the receiver and began speaking. "Branscomb here..."

She'd been so upset she hadn't heard him come in. But she was grateful for his presence, for the silent strength he communicated to her with his nearness. Her fear receded as she listened to his low, calm voice, asking questions, giving orders. She was grateful for his arm supporting her, and though his touch was casual, there was, nevertheless, an implied intimacy in it, a need that was not only her own but his.

When he hung up, he continued to cradle her against him for a long moment. She felt his hands gently moving through the masses of her hair, and she clung to him, holding herself breathlessly still, waiting expectantly for him to speak, not daring to say anything herself for fear that it would be the wrong thing.

"David's in Houston at the bus station, and he thinks Adam's in Houston too," Ross said at last. "But he hasn't found him yet."

"Maybe...I should go back...."

Ross's grip tightened around her waist, and she felt his warm breath shiver softly across her scalp. Her every nerve end was attuned to his male presence. His next words stunned her.

"Not tonight," he said huskily, "not in that red death trap you're driving, when you're frantic about Adam and I've been so rough on you. I know how you drive when you're upset. You could easily wrap that car and yourself around a tree before you get to Beaumont."

He was going to let her stay! Her heart beat wildly with joy even as she attempted to conceal this happiness, forcing herself instead to bristle at his slur against her driving. "I know how to drive!" she snapped, but only half-heartedly.

"Oh, yeah. Why aren't you driving your own car then?" he murmured softly.

Desperately she tried to think up a lie with which to defend herself, but captured as she was against his hard male body, she could scarcely think. She was too disturbingly aware of him as a man. Her normally fertile imagination failed her. "I... It..." She lapsed into a defeated silence, and though a smile tugged at the corners of Ross's mouth as he savored his victory, gallantly he refrained from saying anything more.

For a long time he held her close, her head against his shoulder, her black hair spilling its glistening waves over his arm, and she was achingly aware of every place his body touched hers.

"When that phone rang I knew just how much I needed you here," he said at last, crushing her against him even more tightly so that his lean hard body seemed to imprint itself against her softness. "I was—terrified."

"So was I."

"It's been hell waiting alone," he admitted reluctantly.

His virile charm was working its old magic, and she felt strangely aglow. "I know. I needed to be with you too," she whispered.

"You can sleep in Adam's room," he said thickly, spelling out the sleeping arrangements so that she realized he still had no intention of involving himself with her in a man-woman way, "for tonight."

She swallowed. "All right." She would have agreed to sleeping on the floor, so long as he let her stay.

He laced his larger hand through her tiny one, his warm fingertips possessively pressing against her knuckles, fusing their palms together. "I'm glad you're here," he said slowly, "in spite of what I said earlier. Somehow the waiting gets so much harder at night." He drew her ebony head down against his chest. She heard the steady beat of his heart, and a feeling of infinite peace enveloped them as they held on to each other in the silent house, neither wishing to break the spell that wrapped them.

At last Ross drew away, deliberately setting her from him.

"Why does the house always smell so good when you're in it?" he asked with quiet wonder.

She looked up at him, her lovely face still and radiant. "It's either because I brought some ginger lilies in, or it's the stew I'm cooking."

"I'll go for the stew," Ross said, taking her hand again and leading her toward the kitchen. He lifted the lid on the pot, and his stomach grumbled with enthusiasm as he caught the scent of browned beef and fragrant spices. "What do you say we put dinner on the table—immediately?"

"I'm starving too," she admitted, smiling up at him. "All I've eaten today is a few bites of the pizza that Bruce was sweet enough to bring over this afternoon."

Abruptly Ross released her hand and turned away from her on the pretext of opening the dishwasher so he could remove clean dishes and set the table. Dishes clattered as he began to work furiously. His dark face had grown even darker at Diana's mention of Bruce, for he'd grown unreasonably angry at the thought of Bruce and her together. Dixon's sweetness to *his* wife rankled. He thought of the red Ferrari in his drive beside his own nondescript truck, and suddenly a bolt of intense jealousy shot through him.

Diana, maddeningly unaware of his annoyance, was humming as she shredded a head of lettuce into a wooden salad bowl, sprinkling in grated cheeses and chopped mushrooms. With an effort Ross pushed Dixon from his mind and concentrated on the preparations for supper.

As the two of them sat down at the kitchen table he could not stop himself from noting the excellent and very attractive meal she had put together with only leftovers and a few vegetables, a meal so different from the frozen TV dinners and fast food carryouts he and Adam all too often ate. Sprigs of parsley garnished her tossed green salad; the stew sizzled in its rich gravy. As Ross served first her plate and then his own, he found himself remembering uneasily how comfortable she'd once made his life. She was such a feminine woman, skilled at catering to a man, so talented at making a house a home. She'd been back only two hours, and everything seemed radically different. Suddenly he was acutely conscious of how deeply he had missed her, how poorly he had managed without her. With a start he knew he'd been very unwise to let her stay.

They ate in silence, but it was a companionable silence, the awkwardness having temporarily vanished between them. For the moment Ross had put aside his hostility toward her and had accepted the necessity of her presence so long as Adam was missing. Diana watched with feminine satisfaction when he placed a third helping of roast stew on his plate. It was all too obvious how much he missed her cooking. She sighed. Perhaps one day…

She couldn't help thinking of the night that lay ahead. They would be sleeping in the house where once they'd slept together as man and wife. No matter what Ross had said about their separate sleeping arrangements, he was as keenly conscious of that as she was. From time to time she caught him glancing across the table at her, and though he was valiantly fighting his emotions, he was losing the battle.

A hot dark light burned in the golden depths of his beautiful eyes, and her blood was fired with a passion only he could ignite. Once when their gazes locked, she wondered if his mind was running along the same path as hers, if he were imagining them together in his great king-size bed, their naked bodies curled warmly together as they snuggled beneath sheets and blankets, satiated with lovemaking, wrapped in a sensual, fluid world all their own.

Flustered, she was the one who suddenly looked away from the hunger she saw in his bold, hot eyes, her black lashes demurely fluttering down against the crimson warmth of her cheeks. Strange emotions overwhelmed her, and she felt foolish and gauche, afraid suddenly to speak for fear of stammering and revealing her complete vulnerability.

With a groan he wrenched himself from the table, feeling ridiculous himself, as though he were a schoolboy again unable to make conversation with a virgin. She was, after all, his estranged wife, a woman he was determined to put aside! He was a man nearing forty, old enough to consider consequences before he entered into a relationship.

Without saying a word he strode from the room. He felt acute self-disgust. He wanted her; he'd never stopped wanting her. She was in his blood, the delicious taste of her, the feel of her silken flesh, her sweet, womanly scent. Every fiber in his being ached for her, for she was as much a part of him as the forest and bayous he loved, as his son Adam. In that moment he knew what he'd always known—that he couldn't live without her.

But he was determined to try.

she did was busy work, and she performed the tasks mechanically, her mind numb with worry about Adam and despair over Ross.

After the dishwasher ceased its gurgling and churning, she became deeply conscious of Ross's every movement in the den, of the low blurred drone of the television, of the flick of his lighter when he lit a cigarette. It was obvious he couldn't concentrate on any one show; he switched channels repeatedly, finally turning the television off entirely and going to his bedroom.

When at last she dared venture into the den she saw that he'd brought her suitcase inside. It stood in the middle of the room looking lost and lonely, like an unwelcome guest. Picking it up, she carried it into Adam's room and decided to get ready for bed. Quickly she stripped out of her jeans and lavender blouse and took a long sudsy shower in Adam's private bath, washing her hair and toweling it dry. Then she pulled on her favorite, smotheringly voluminous granny gown, an item of apparel that Ross had always hated. It was a shapeless garment with nothing to recommend it other than its familiarity and comfort, its brilliant red having long ago faded to a dull shade of pink. Once when she'd worn it Ross had teasingly chided, "Why does a woman of your impeccable taste put on something that ugly when she's about to sleep with her husband?" He'd laughed then. "It must be because you know I'll rip it off you if you don't take it off yourself and sleep naked beside me," he'd continued with a chuckle, his eyes glinting with amusement.

Blue eyes sparkling, she'd darted coyly away from him and slipped hurriedly out of the gown. When he'd pulled her into his arms, his hard throbbing masculine need pressing against the naked flesh of her lower belly, she'd giggled lightly, her breath falling warmly against his throat, betraying her own eagerness. "Sometimes I think that's the sexiest gown I have...."

"I think you're right," he'd murmured as his lips lovingly nibbled the hollow between her breasts, before they'd surrendered to the swirling rapture of their love. "I won't ever let you wear it more than five seconds."

Diana pushed the pleasant memory from her mind and slipped into Adam's narrow twin bed. The mattress felt hard and unfamiliar, the sheets stiff and musty, the pillow too soft. Even as she switched off the bedside lamp, she knew that she would be awake for hours.

Pale silver moonlight sifted through the trees, casting a bar of white brilliance against a Garfield poster that hung against the far wall. The enormous orange cat smirked rebelliously. Suddenly Diana was near tears as she thought of Adam and how crazily enthusiastic he'd been about that comic strip cat the last time he'd visited her. She'd spoiled him by buying three of the latest Garfield books he'd been wild to have, and she saw them stacked neatly on his desk beside his bed. If anything happened to her darling, precious little boy...

In her mind's eye she saw the frenzied race of traffic upon the Houston freeways, the snarled congestion of the older sections of town, the maze of construction and the glamorous high rises massed in the Southwest. And her child was lost in that vast, bewildering city.... How would a mere ten-year-old find his way around? She thought of the disheveled indigents that filled the city. There were so many desperate, homeless people who, having heard rumors of Houston's wealth, had poured into the city. What if he met the wrong one?...

She sat bolt upright in bed, terrified. Nervously her hand curled the sheet, knotting it in her shaking fingers. Then she forced her mind to blot out the nightmarish horror that was threatening to swamp her. He had to be all right! He just had to be. She said a long, silent prayer, and lay back feeling vaguely calmed.

Hours passed, and she drifted in and out of sleep, her tortured dreams returning her to consciousness. Then, exhausted, she would fall asleep again.

At first it seemed that she dreamed that a phone was ringing. Then she was snapped brutally awake by her fear, the sound all too jarringly real, its clamor punctuating the hushed silence of the house. She heard the last tingle of a ring as Ross answered it in his bedroom down the hall.

Terror made her blood run hot and cold and sent tremors racing through her as she threw the sheets aside with one fumbling motion and stumbled from the bed, haltingly tripping over something Adam had left on the floor. She raced down the hall to Ross's bedroom and threw open the door, stepping fearfully inside.

Her heart beat a wild and painful tattoo in her throat, and she brought her hand to her mouth, chewing on her bared knuckles, her mind seething in an agony of suspense as she listened to the low resonance of Ross's voice. How could he speak so calmly when she felt she was falling to pieces?

Everything seemed so unreal in the silvery darkness, like a shadowy dream. She moved toward the bed, sinking down beside Ross, her hand unconsciously seeking his beneath the covers and holding on to it tightly as she listened.

"Just a minute," Ross said into the receiver. Then she was aware of his arms circling her protectively, pulling her gently to him. "He's all right, Diana," Ross whispered fiercely against her soft, tear-stained cheek. "David's found Adam."

"Oh, thank God!" she murmured, tears of joy and relief spilling from her thick lashes, hysterical laughter bubbling softly in her throat as she clung to him.

Smoothing tumbling raven tresses from her face, Ross leaned over and kissed Diana very tenderly on the lips. It was a wondrous, magical moment.

She continued to sob softly—quiet, joyous tears.

"Don't cry, my darling. Adam's safe," he whispered. "Safe...."

She tried to smile for him but couldn't. Ross was being infinitely kind. In gratitude her fingertips reached up and brushed his sensual lips, her light touch the gentlest of caresses as she reverently outlined the shape of his mouth. She was aware of his lips hovering breathtakingly close to her own, aware too of the sandpaper texture of his masculine cheek as her hand stroked it, tracing the hard line of his jaw.

Still cradling Diana against him, Ross picked up the phone again. Diana could scarcely concentrate on what he said, and she caught only snatches. But she knew enough. Adam was sound asleep on Bruce's couch, and David was going to bring him home to Orange first thing in the morning.

When Ross hung up, he held her silent, shaking body against his, his own relief as overwhelmingly intense as hers. He wanted her near him. She was the one person on earth who was in tune with him emotionally at that moment, who could relate to the hell he'd been through. He hadn't known how great his fear was until he'd tasted the sweetness of relief.

Gently he gave her the details about Adam, but her mind seemed unable to retain anything he said unless he repeated himself again and again. Then he promised to explain everything in the morning.

What Ross didn't tell her was that he had wanted to go after his son himself at once, but that David had talked him out of it, explaining that when Adam had found out Diana was in Orange, Adam wanted nothing more than to return home and find his parents together. Ross had agreed, not only because of his son's request, but for his own selfish reasons. It would be much easier to confront Adam again with Diana at his side. She was a woman, and she had a mysterious feminine ability to buffer the tensions of his relationship with Adam before they got out of control. Never before had Ross known how much Adam missed and needed his mother, nor how much easier his role as a father was when she was at his side.

He still loved Diana, and for the moment this thought robbed him of his remorseless desire to force her out of his life. When he'd cradled her quivering body in his arms and she'd wept with happiness and relief, he'd learned how much he cared.

Ross held her gently against his great relaxed body, stroking her. She felt so small and feminine against him; he savored the feel of her, wanting to protect her. Though he knew it was madness to go on holding her, he couldn't stop himself. He'd been alone—without a woman—for too long. She was his wife, the most beautiful woman he'd ever known, and he was only a man.

"Diana...." Her name on his lips was low and husky, and he knew she sensed at once his change in mood. She knew he wanted her.

"Hmmm...." She breathed, sounding coyly distant, though he'd felt the immediate quickening of her pulse.

He turned his face toward hers so that his breath whispered softly against her cheek. "I think...under the circumstances...we should reconsider the wisdom of our sleeping arrangements," he murmured, a low chuckle in his throat. "Since Adam's coming home tomorrow...and he'll be needing his own room..."

Lazily she cut him off, her tone seductively teasing. "We have something wonderful we need to celebrate, don't we, Ross." Her hand played through his black hair at the base of his neck, twirling a raven strand around her littlest finger. "What do you suppose we could do to..." She let her words trail off. Her brilliant eyes, alight with tempestuous anticipation, swept downward over the hard muscles of his bare chest and the flat of his belly. "What...could we do to celebrate?"

Suddenly he felt hot all over. "Don't ask a question when you already know the answer."

"But some questions...are such fun to think about," she returned playfully.

"Maybe the answer will be even more fun...than thinking about the question." His low sexy chuckle vibrated through her. "Wanton..."

"Only with you...." she whispered. "Oh, Ross," she murmured against his roughened cheek. "I'm so happy. So thankfully happy...."

"So am I, love."

For the first time in three years they had turned to each other in their need, and each had supported the other. They clung to each other, not thinking beyond the physical comfort they found in the other's nearness.

He could feel the tantalizingly rounded curves of her slim body beneath the thin material of her gown, the warmth of her pressed against him. Her presence in his bed stirred too many pleasant, erotic memories for him to send her away, and he'd known the minute she'd stepped inside his bedroom, looking so young and sweetly vulnerable in her shapeless, frumpty nightgown, that gown that had always been a source of amusement between them, that he could no longer stay his need of her.

"I want you, Diana," he murmured thickly. "You've won. I haven't the strength to fight my desire for you any longer."

"As long as you have the strength to...you know..." Her low voice was huskily suggestive, her luminous smile alluring. Tossing her head playfully, she concealed her hurt at his previous remark, for she understood too well why he felt reluctant to simply take her. A velvet fingertip slowly traced a tantalizing line downward across bronzed muscles, through the mat of black curling hairs, down the length of his male torso, lifting her hand at the last moment in a modest, delicate feminine gesture, little guessing how wild she'd driven him.

"Don't you worry about me having that kind of strength," he muttered fiercely, his control ragged as he pulled her to him.

Her blood surged, her pulsebeats hammering against her eardrum as she caught the urgency of his passion in his deep tone. "I love you, Ross...."

"Don't speak to me of love," he ground out, stiffening, his old bitterness suddenly upon him. "I'm a man. You're a woman. Let's keep things simple between us."

If only she could... Her heart cried out in pain, but she lay against the pillows, her smile having vanished, her lips compressed, uttering not a sound, keeping her sadness inside.

"I don't like...to say things to hurt you, Diana," he said more gently at last. "You know that."

"Yes, I know..." she murmured, trying to swallow against a lump that had grown painful in her throat. She should be grateful he was sensitive to her feelings and content that he still wanted her.

Very gently Ross ran his fingers through the perfumed sweetness of her loosened hair, which flowed like rich black silken waves upon his pillow, and then nuzzled his lips against the warm sensitive flesh at the nape of her neck. A man could lose himself in such a woman.

Ignoring her inner pain, she nestled against him, shaping her body so provocatively to his that he groaned aloud. She was a temptress, intuitively pleasing him, arousing him until he was insane with need. When his mouth covered hers, he felt her lips quivering beneath his in response. She opened her mouth so that his tongue could easily push inside into the damp warm depths, the heat of her tongue sliding against his like molten satin.

Wrapping her with his arms, he buried his face beneath her hair, trailing his lips across her throat, the moist hot touch of his mouth like a tiny flame erotically searing love-sensitized skin until she was whimpering and straining toward his lips.

He pushed the soft fabric of her gown upward to her shoulders until the cloth bunched above her taut nipples, revealing her lush beauty in intimate display.

Then with a quick jerking motion he pulled the garment from her body and thrust it savagely onto the carpet.

She pressed her breasts and her loins against him, and he reveled in the sensation of the graceful length of her flesh against his. His desire grew so acute that inarticulate love words were wrenched unwillingly from his soul before he silenced himself by smothering her lips with his in a long and bruising kiss. With his tongue he forced her mouth open, and the fire that was consuming him swept through her, making them both tremble as they held one another.

Suddenly a strange anger coursed through him, anger that he was so possessed by this woman he'd determined to put out of his life, and his mouth ravished hers, exploring, demanding, plundering. Her sweetness made his pulse race, her wantonness inflamed him. His hands moved down against her belly, flicking lightly around her navel, erotically toying with it, driving her mad with his delicate touching, trailing lower, his expert fingers caressing the softest flesh of her inner thighs where they parted.

She gasped, the unexpected intimacy of his touch sending such an unbearable thrill through her that she tried to retreat from the exquisite torture of the blazing sensations he aroused. He swung one leg heavily across her, holding her down, easily trapping her beneath him so that he could continue his exploration, his hand delicately manipulating the secret folds of her damp flesh, rousing her fully.

"Don't, Ross," she pleaded breathlessly, brushing

futilely against his expert fingers. "I feel crazy when you do that...."

"Pleasantly crazy, I hope," he murmured.

"I can't think...I can't breathe."

"I don't want you to think," he muttered roughly. "I want you to feel...like you make me feel."

His tone of voice made her vaguely unhappy, for as always he sounded as though he wanted to have nothing to do with her. She continued to struggle, lashing out with her fists, pushing at the hard mass of his body leaning against hers, kicking out with her feet. But he was far more powerful than she. Her feet merely became tangled in the sheets, her blows were weak and ineffectual against his strength. Effortlessly he held her beneath him, her movements and faint passionate whimperings only increasing his masculine need; her building excitement only arousing him further. When at last she thought she could stand the dizzying, pleasurable sensations no longer, he withdrew his hand. Negligently he lay back upon the mattress and pulled her down on top of him, holding her supple female body above his for a long, suspended moment, his avid male gaze admiring the pendulous globes of soft feminine flesh and the tininess of her waist where his hands spanned her.

He could see the startled wild light in her wide blue eyes as he slowly eased her body down. A pagan shiver ran through him at the first warm enveloping contact with her, and to savor the incredible warmth that wrapped him, he held her body motionless upon his own.

In that first glorious moment of complete intimacy, Diana gazed down through the delicate fans of her thick sable lashes into Ross's desire-darkened eyes. The frozen instant of captured time was one of hushed stillness for them both. Her expression was filled with yearning and love, and she knew that the depths of her soul were bared to him, his loving assault having crumbled all her defenses. It was what she wanted— for him to know how desperately she loved him, how completely she was his, that it was his love that she wanted as well as his lovemaking. She could no more live without being emotionally bonded to this man than she could live without the touch of his hands upon her secret flesh and the union of their bodies when he was within her. She hoped with all her heart that he would believe what he saw and learn to trust her again.

"Oh, Ross...Ross...Ross..."

He ripped his eyes from her luminous features, not wanting to face the deep emotions he saw written there. Instead he savagely crushed his mouth against the swollen softness of her lips once and then again, holding her tightly to him, lost himself in the wild pagan thrill of the primitive urges that devoured him.

They fitted tightly together, as only a man fits the woman he loves, mating with the same wonder as the joining of the last two pieces of a puzzle, two souls joined in the vast pattern of the universe. He made love to her fiercely, selfishly taking all that she offered. Her head was bent low over his, her long black hair brushing back and forth against his lips in swift, feather-light strokes.

Again and again she cried his name as warm currents of desire stirred within her, wracking her with violent waves of burning need, eclipsing at last in a meteoric burst of flaming sensations. But he waited to take his own pleasure, holding himself back so that he could bring her time after time to shattering fulfillment.

Suddenly she felt the unbelievable fire of him; it was like a fever burning him first and then searing her own flesh as well until they were both consumed by its obliterating force. She was soft and pliant in his arms, clasping the sinewed muscles of his perspiration-dampened back fiercely, her wanton responsiveness evoking even greater heights of passion from him. Diana clung to Ross in a frenzy of hope and need, withholding nothing, giving herself to him recklessly and with complete abandon, longing for him to admit that his need for her was as great as hers for him, wanting him, needing him so desperately.

His hard warm hands drifted over her rounded breasts to her slim waist, and then as his own passion seized him, he pulled her hips tightly against himself as he shuddered within her warm fluid velvet flesh. In that last unguarded moment he was in the grip of feelings so powerful that he would have cried out the three words she would have given anything to hear had his mouth not been passionately fused to hers, his tongue inside her, mating wetly with her own.

Instead he collapsed beside her, his head against

her warm cheek, his strength ebbing slowly, his body's need assuaged. As he stared at her silent form beside him, his mind was a welcome hollow of all emotion; he did not want to dwell on the knowledge of her power over him, of how completely she could wrest him from himself. There had been no barriers between them when he'd made love to her, but slowly, as his passion drained, he fell comfortably back into himself.

Diana lay quietly within the curve of Ross's strong arms, the tremblings of their bodies having stilled. Her blue eyes opened drowsily, her eyelids heavy with delightful, languorous memory, her lips curving gently in languid contentment. She was aware of Ross's silence, of the absence of loving words, but she was too aglow to worry. What they had had together was enough.

Tenderly Ross's hands tightened about her shoulders as she snuggled even more closely against him. He thought her beautiful. Never had he thought her more so, her slender face flushed even in the silvery moonlight, her dark hair a tangle of gleaming waves upon his pillow. Quietly he watched her until her eyes closed and her breathing slowed into a regular murmur. Then he too drifted into sleep, holding her in his arms, not wanting to let her go.

Soft, reddish-gold sunlight splashed through the long, narrow windows, lighting with its brilliance the familiar furnishings of the bedroom—the gleaming brass headboard against the wall, the narrowly striped beige wallpaper and the old-fashioned quilts piled on top of the sleeping woman who had burrowed beneath them to escape the unwelcome light.

Diana awakened slowly, cupping her mouth daintily with her hands as she yawned. Outside the world seemed to be holding its breath, not a creature stirring amidst the brown leaves littering the long grasses nor a bird fluttering in the low branches of the trees. The dark woods were wrapped in hushed, early-morning stillness.

Vaguely conscious of the too-silent house, Diana stretched luxuriantly, reaching across the bed for Ross to discover that his side of the bed was no more than a cool tumble of sheets. His absence brought her sharply awake, a nagging sense of loss filling her. When they'd lived together, he'd always lingered to hold her and kiss her good morning.

She sat up in bed, her back sinking against her soft pillow, her bare shoulders prickling with goose bumps in the cool morning air. Shivering with cold and feeling heavy with sleep, as though she'd slept too deeply and too long, she bundled the sheets up to her neck and lay back, feeling cozy at last, her thoughts drifting in a scrambled, languid daze before turning to Ross.

Things were very different between Ross and her now, she thought with a pang of sorrow. She knew he was reluctant to involve himself with her again and suspected that that was the reason he'd left as soon as he'd gotten up. Perhaps he had decided that he would have nothing more to do with her. But when she thought of his passionate lovemaking last night, she doubted that. A tiny satisfied smile curved her lips, soothing away the tiny frown of worry. Perhaps she was closer to winning Ross than he was ready to admit. "Patience," she whispered to herself. "Patience...." But it was so difficult to hold herself in check and give him the time he needed.

Deciding to get up, she swung her bare feet over the edge of the bed and reached toward the faded pink tangle of cloth pooled on the carpet and pulled the nightgown over her shoulders. It felt cool and soft against her warm skin, and she hugged herself tightly, smiling again, remembering the wanton splendor of the night before. Maybe this was indeed the sexiest nightgown she owned....

Half an hour later found her in the kitchen briskly and efficiently brewing coffee and squeezing orange juice. Ross was gone and so was his truck. Sections of *The Orange Leader* were scattered on the kitchen table as though he'd begun to read it and hadn't been able to concentrate. A single cigarette had been impatiently stubbed in the ashtray.

Diana poured herself a cup of coffee and stared uncomfortably at the newspaper, not liking the thought that she'd driven Ross from his own home. She felt restlessly at loose ends but too lazy and tired to want to do anything constructive. It was a long time before she was able to summon the self-discipline Madelaine had so carefully instilled and talk herself into using his absence to advantage by defrosting a chicken in the microwave, making Ross's favorite casserole for lunch, cleaning house and filling vases with the flowers she loved. All these things she at last accomplished in a desultory fashion.

She was outside, indifferently potting several lush ferns to bring into the house, when an unfamiliar white Chevrolet bounced up the road and then braked in front of the house. Glad of any excuse to quit her work and hopeful that it would be Ross, she rose slowly to her knees, her hands and fingernails grimy with potting soil, and stared in confusion at the strange car. When the car door was thrust open and a dark-haired boy leaped out, his red shirt a flash of brilliance as he ran toward her shouting her name, her slender face was suddenly illuminated with a fiercely wild joy that matched his. Adam flung himself into her waiting arms, and her tears of joy dampened his black hair as she held him tightly, her soiled hands leaving dark marks on the back of his red shirt.

Gravel crunched beneath tires as an approaching truck slowed behind the Chevrolet, but for a long time neither mother nor son were aware of anything except their own joyful reunion. Beneath towering moss-draped cypress trees and the sweetly smelling, sough-ing pines, everything had come right in Diana's world again. At last Diana's gaze swung to the three silent men, Ross, David, and Bruce, standing near the Chev-rolet together, and she was acutely conscious of them watching her.

Ross looked so very alone, so uncomfortably left out. He needed to hold Adam and rejoice as she was doing, and yet because of his pride deliberately kept his distance. His proud, aloof stance caught at her heart. Slowly she loosened her arms around her son and drew herself to her full height. Her gentle eyes left Ross and sought Adam's once again, this time beseechingly.

"Adam...son, your dad's here. He..."

Adam's black eyes darkened imperceptibly, and when he spoke, his one word was stubbornly indifference. "Yeah...." His small hand gripped his mother's with increased tension as he cast a sideways glance toward his father.

"He's been so worried about you, Adam," she whispered coaxingly. "We both have. He loves you. Please...won't you go to him?..."

"I...I can't," was all he said, very softly. He stood rigidly beside her. "I was running away from him."

"Please...for my sake."

Black, defiant eyes held hers for a long moment as Adam hesitated, his young mind a turmoil of indecision. Then the smoldering light was banked, his mulish expression gentling.

Adam shrugged. "Okay, if it's really what you want."

She held on to him fiercely. "I want us to be a family again, and this could be the first step." Something flashed in his dark eyes, a tiny ray of flaring longing, but it vanished as quickly as it had appeared. It was as if, unlike her, he didn't dare to allow himself to hope.

She watched him, her heart aching with trepidation as Adam walked with stiff reluctance toward his father. Ross, his dark face just as stubbornly unreadable as his son's, left the men to meet Adam halfway. When they reached each other Ross knelt, his denim knee crushing the thick, damp grasses, taking his son in his arms. For a long intense time he held Adam silently.

A fierce emotion gripped Ross that shook him to the core of his being. He had been very afraid he'd lose this child as he had lost everyone else he'd ever loved. He could still lose him if he didn't learn to change, and he wasn't sure he could—without Diana. Was he rationalizing, pretending that he needed her for his son and not himself? It didn't matter. In that moment he conceded to himself that he wasn't going to send her away, even though he knew he probably should.

As if in a dream Diana was aware of them beckoning her to join them, of her body somehow moving slowly toward them though her legs felt numb. But it was no dream when Ross's hand wrapped itself around hers, searing her flesh with its vibrant contact.

Adam looked up, staring at his parents, not understanding the strangeness of adult ways. His parents had been enemies for so long—he couldn't credit the warmth in his father's eyes, nor the new softness in his mother.

"Will you let Mother stay with us?" Adam asked, wanting to be certain of what he thought.

"If she will," Ross said hoarsely. "I never realized how much you missed her." Very deliberately he omitted his own needs where she was concerned, his conscience stabbing him when he caught the quick look of pain in her blue eyes before she answered.

"Yes," she whispered gently, "I'll stay."

For a time the three of them were aware only of the happiness of at last finding one another again.

Practical and realistic concerns intervened all too quickly. Ross had to handle Bruce and David while Diana led Adam inside to his room to bathe and change. Bruce had driven over with David so that Diana wouldn't be faced with driving back to Houston alone.

As always, Bruce's thoughtfulness toward Diana goaded Ross, and he was less generous toward the man than he deserved. Ross was sheepishly aware of a certain possessive relish in his tone and an excessive amount of enthusiasm when he slammed the Ferrari door, finally shutting Bruce inside for his drive back to Houston. "Thanks anyway for loaning Diana your car and offering to drive her home," he attempted casually. Ross forced himself to smile at the distinguished man, and Bruce negligently started the car, vaguely amused at the situation.

"My pleasure," Bruce said off-handedly, smiling with genuine warmth, secretly flattered that a man like Ross was so obviously jealous of him.

"I'll be driving Diana over myself in a couple of days so she can get her things and arrange her business affairs," Ross asserted in a deliberate manner that staked his claim.

"I wish you two the best of luck." There was the faintest trace of speculative interest in his tone.

The remark hung in the air between them, a symbol of the uncertainty of the future.

Then Bruce's gaze swung to the house, and he grinned, waving jauntily toward Diana, who'd opened a second-story window and was leaning fetchingly out of it to bid him good-bye. "Pretty girl," he said with frank admiration, his tone deliberately calculated to make Ross's blood boil. "Treat her right this time—or you'll have me to answer to. My second wife was about her age."

Ross didn't know Bruce well enough to recognize the glint of amusement in his gray eyes, and his own angry retort was lost as Bruce deliberately revved his motor. Then in a fierce burst of speed and eruption of gravel Bruce was gone, his sports car a vivid red blur tailed with a white plume of dust, disappearing into the dark fold of trees, the roar of the car fading almost instantly.

Ross jammed his hands into the pockets of his jeans and stared angrily after the other man for a long moment. Bruce was exactly the kind of man Madelaine would have wanted for Diana, a man of enormous wealth and prestigious social stature. But Diana had chosen him over Bruce or a man similar to Bruce. She had lived in Houston for three years without becoming involved with anyone else. That could be a sign that she'd never completely rejected her marriage, though her rejection had felt complete at the time. Relaxing at last, Ross strode carelessly toward the house.

The rest of the day was taken up with settling Adam back into his routine, each parent playing a part, though neither had anything to do with the other. Diana sensed that Ross was deliberately avoiding intimate contact with her. He was letting her stay as his wife, but she was aware that a vast barrier remained between them. She'd lost Ross's trust, and it wasn't going to be easy to regain it.

Thus, she devoted herself to Adam, blotting out her anxieties about her more complicated relationship with Ross. Adam had missed one school day, so after lunch Diana made him sit down at his desk amidst an untidy stack of school books, pencils and rulers and begin his homework. She pulled a chair up beside his and sifted through the tattered and very disorganized pages of his notebook, her frown deepening as she did so. Adam was indifferently scribbling math answers, not concentrating on his work at all, asking every five minutes or so to be excused until, at what must have been his tenth request to go to the bathroom, her patience snapped. "No! You're not getting up again until you finish at least two pages of problems."

"But…"

"No more excuses. You're going to be in real trouble fast if you don't turn over a new leaf."

After she checked his papers she was appalled to note that his obvious reluctance for the task was because he was so far behind—more than one day. She quickly realized that he hadn't been applying himself at all the first few weeks of school, probably a result of his unhappiness. His papers were sloppy and half-finished. To make matters worse he'd fallen into the lazy habit of simply making up answers rather than looking them up when he didn't know them.

Thus, all through that Sunday afternoon as Ross sat poring over his own work at his desk in the den, the sounds of his family's voices drifted down to him; Diana's gentle explanations quickly followed by Adam's murmurs of protest and, when overridden with severe lectures, his sighs of intense frustration. For once Ross was glad she was occupied with Adam and he didn't have to face her or his feelings. In the past Ross had considered her too conscientious and over-protective as a mother. But today he welcomed this flaw, for it afforded him an avenue of escape from his conflicting emotions.

Later that night when Adam was safely asleep in his own bedroom, Ross and Diana lay in bed without speaking, neither daring to touch on their problems. Instead they savored with exquisite, passionate delight the anticipation of making love. They were aware of a quiet shared happiness and that there was no need to rush; they had the whole night before them. Indeed, if they were fortunate, many future nights.

The bed dipped as Diana leaned toward the lamp on the nightstand to extinguish it, and before she succeeded Ross caught her to him, rolling over, bringing her softness hard against his body so that she was directly beneath him. His warm breath gently tickled her face, and she wrinkled her nose. His sensual mouth hovered a mere inch above hers.

"I was only going to put out the light," she murmured in breathless confusion, not understanding.

Amber eyes traced the femaleness of her body, clad only in transparent gold, with avid masculine interest.

"Leave it on," he commanded. "I want to see you—" his eyes glowed intensely "—every inch of you."

For some reason she felt very vulnerable beneath his steady, intent gaze, and she had a coward's desire to hide. "Ross, we always turn out the light." Stubbornly she reached toward it again.

"I didn't realize it was such an entrenched habit," he said dryly, a chuckle deep in his throat. He seized her hand just as her fingertips touched the edge of the dangling chain beneath the silk shade. Slowly he drew her hand to his lips to blow warm kisses between her fingers until she tingled all over with vibrant excitement. "That's all the more reason to leave it on," he murmured coaxingly, inserting his tongue intimately between her fingers, caressingly moving it back and forth against her softest flesh. "We don't want sex to become stale and predictable."

She smiled up at him, her eyes locking with his, her defiance ebbing. "For some reason I've never worried about that...with you," she said huskily. She wound and unwound a strip of his raven hair around trembling fingertips.

"Nor with anyone else, I hope," he stated with

gruff possessiveness, pulling her completely beneath him, pinioning her, dominating her with his great muscular body so that she could not escape him. She was pleasantly aware of the weight of his body molding itself to hers, of the bristly black hairs of his bronzed chest tickling her breasts, of the long sweep of his muscular thighs on either side of her legs. For a long time he stared deeply into her eyes.

Then at last his head lowered to hers, his parted lips moving gently across the swollen softness of hers, forcing her mouth open, teasing her senses with slow, wet, languorous touches. He could feel the beginnings of her response to him, the heat of her, the tiny tremors that shook her. Beneath his lips, hers were sensitive quivering flesh, their velvet softness meeting his in tantalizing union, meltingly warm. He felt the violent throbbing of her pulse when his mouth lowered to kiss her throat.

Slowly he loosed the tiny buttons on the front of her silken gown, his long fingers sliding inside to brush the button tips of her nipples until they were taut with arousal. He was glad her vanity had made her forsake her frumpy pink garment of the night before for this gown of delicate coppery satin that shimmered like glowing fire in the silvery moonlight and clung to her body like an outer layer of transparent silken skin, enhancing her feminine shapeliness. Expertly he pulled it over her creamy shoulders, its silky texture sliding erotically over the softest places of her body. Carelessly he tossed it toward the foot of the bed, where it landed on the mound of bunched covers they'd pushed aside earlier.

For a long moment of suspended time he stared wondrously into the glowing depths of her eyes. Neither of them spoke with words, though they spoke to each other with their eyes and smiles in the silent language of lovers. Finally she clasped her arms together about his broad warm back, feeling the smooth ripple of his muscles beneath her hands as she pulled him against her hot nude body with wanton purpose, her curves fitting the hard outline of him with such rightness that in that moment he knew she was completely his.

That night he took her again and again, each time losing himself in the needs of his flesh, wanting to reassure himself that he had her in his house, in his bed. He had to know that she was really his once again, wanting to banish in a frenzied haze of reckless desire all his doubts for their future happiness.

Diana loved him hopelessly, gloriously, incoherently, as he brought her time after time to brilliant crests of pleasure. She was his, and someday soon, he would be hers as totally as she was his…she hoped.…

Despite their passionate physical reunion, despite their silent protestations that they would find lasting happiness together, in the deepest recess of their minds perplexing emotions invaded their subconscious, and neither could be sure of the other.

Eight

Diana leaned toward the mirror, squinting at her reflection in concentration as she secured the solitary pearl earring to her earlobe. The tiny gold back suddenly skittered through her trembling fingers, a glittering speck falling through the air, disappearing into the deep brown carpet at her feet. She stared down at the floor in frustration, searching for it, thinking as she did so that she wasn't usually this clumsy. It was just that she'd become very nervous this afternoon when she'd talked to her mother on the phone. At first there had only been the faintest hint of disapproval in her mother's cool, restrained tone. But when Diana had tried to explain why she'd gone back to Ross, her mother had become openly furious.

* * *

"Darling! I hope you don't mind my saying…"

Diana had smelled trouble instantly at the phrase *I hope you don't mind my saying,* for Madelaine always prefaced all criticisms by politely cloaking them with courteous mishmash. Her mother could handily rip a person to shreds with her sugary-sharp tongue and ready advice, but she did so with an amiable smile, cherishing the notion that a true Southern lady such as herself was never openly discourteous, but rather constructively critical. Thus, it was her peculiar code of chivalry to excuse herself politely before she poked her long nose into another's business.

Her mother's conversation whirled in Diana's mind.

"Darling! I hope you don't mind my saying… You've always been a little fool where Ross is concerned! I couldn't believe it when Hazel told me you'd been living with him for three whole weeks!"

"Four, Mother," Diana had stated flatly. "And as for *living with him,* he is my husband!"

"An absurd mistake you should have corrected two years ago. Why didn't I insist that you divorce him? I should have known something like this could still happen. Ross can be so overbearing—forgive me, dear—but you're always so spineless when he is…even though it makes you miserable. I should never have gone to Europe.…" Madelaine paused and took a deep, much-needed breath, as though her heart were fluttering wildly in her agitation and she had to calm herself. "Excuse me for asking this, Diana, but are you still so naive as to believe the two of you can live together with even a degree of compatibility? Why, you are as different as night and day! A marriage between you two is even worse than mating my adorable, pampered Persian, Sylvie, to that dreadful Rhodesian Ridgeback at the end of the block. The only thing they could possibly have in common is the color of their fur! Why, that monster gobbles cats alive whenever he gets the chance!''

A vision of poor, gobbled Sylvie was scarcely heartwarming.

"Really, Mother! If it makes you feel better, I didn't have a single tooth mark last night when I checked myself before I took a bath.''

"Good grief! Don't be so literal! I didn't mean Ross physically hurts you! He's much too clever for that. Perhaps I shouldn't say this, but he's sadistic. Just think about the way Ross forces you to live out there in that dreadful house, so far from town, when he knows how you hate being so alone out in the forest. When he knows…it frightens you. I wouldn't call that kind. It's deliberate cruelty. And another point that I hate to bring up—I can't help worrying constantly about the way he wants to just let Adam run wild. Why, the poor child doesn't have a shred of discipline. Adam could run away from home, and I doubt if his father would miss him for days.'' Madelaine had hesitated, but not for lack of purpose, merely to let what she considered her excellent arguments sink in. Little did she know how deeply she'd upset Diana by mentioning the possibility of Adam running away, unerringly hitting a vulnerable nerve, even though Diana and Ross had not told her about the incident.

Madelaine's voice seemed to go and on. "I don't want to be critical, but you must admit that Ross has always been so absurd when it comes to money. Do you remember his rudeness to me when I gave you a washer and dryer when you were first married so you wouldn't have to drive all those miles into town to that horrid Laundromat? I was only trying to be helpful, and I'll never forget how unbelievably insulting he was when I tried to insist that he let you keep them. Why, it took me simply hours and hours to return them, and did he care about the trouble he put me to? I hate to say this, but he has never shown me the slightest consideration!"

"Maybe, Mother, Ross wouldn't have been so unreasonably proud if you hadn't put it into everyone's mind that he married me for my money!" Diana snapped heatedly, her own fury rising. "You've never liked him because he won't let you run over him!" For a moment there she had felt like a child again, defending herself and her marriage to her domineering mother.

"I was only trying to point out..."

"Mother," Diana growled, "stop trying to run my life!"

"I'm sure I never wanted to do that," her mother purred.

Madelaine had backed down at once, weeping at least a teaspoonful of alligator tears, sweetly apologizing. But Diana knew she was like a crafty general

who was merely retreating and retrenching to think
her strategy through and find a better line of attack,
her first seeming to have failed.

But in reality it had not failed, for after Madelaine
had hung up, Diana had been very depressed. Their
thirty-minute conversation had left her shaking and
her head pulsating with blinding shafts of pain. Everything that Madelaine said was all too true.

In the month that she'd lived with Ross, Diana had
had to bite her tongue hundreds of times to keep their
arguments at a minimum. If she hadn't, they would
have been fighting constantly. Ross was emphatically
against her asking her father for a second loan to start
a branch of her business in Orange, and this was
something she wanted very much to be able to do.
Though Ross was willing to finance her venture himself on a less elaborate scale than she would have
liked, he wouldn't have the money available until after the first of the year. Until then she felt like she
was twiddling her thumbs and accomplishing very little. In the meantime she was forced to go back and
forth to Houston to see about her unresolved affairs
there. Usually she worked all day Wednesday in
Houston, spent the night there, worked the next day,
and drove home Thursday evening.

Then there was the matter of how she and Ross felt
about Adam. Ross wanted his son to learn to be independent. Ross favored letting the boy spend nights
with his friends, go camping, find his own way to and
from school, and do his schoolwork on his own, even
if this meant lower grades. And, indeed, Adam was

used to doing these things. While Diana, using the excuse that she'd missed Adam these past three years, said she wanted him home, close to her. She always had a reason why Adam should stay home instead of visiting his friends, why she should take him to school instead of letting him ride his bike, why just this once she needed to help him with his homework. She kept thinking that later she would feel differently, and it would be easier to accept him being an independent young man. But for now, he seemed so young. She knew that this tug of war was even harder on Adam than it was on his parents, but she couldn't stop herself from feeling as she did.

Diana had been trying much too hard to maintain a calm facade in her relationship with Ross, but she was terribly afraid for the future. She kept wondering if Ross wanted her to postpone starting her business to see if things were going to work out between them. Perhaps he didn't want her establishing herself permanently in Orange if they weren't going to be together. If he still had doubts about their future, would he find some new excuse after the first of the year?

But in spite of their problems she was glad to be home. Orange hadn't changed much during her absence, and small-town life suited her better than the hectic pace of Houston. There might not be as much to do, but what there was, was more deeply pleasurable. One afternoon she'd enjoyed taking Adam to see a Western art collection in the Stark Museum. Like all boys his age, he preferred outdoor trips. Frequently she and Ross took him bass fishing and crawfishing in their favorite spots near the Sabine River. Once the three of them had borrowed a friend's airboat to explore the marshes and observe the wildlife, and she'd even thought it fun when the engine had died, and they'd had to tramp back through mud and mush, leading the boat behind them. Just being home with the man she loved was wonderful.

In the evenings there was horse racing to be enjoyed at Delta Downs Racetrack in nearby Vinton, Louisiana, or an occasional road show at the new Frances Ann Lutcher Theater downtown.

The physical side of her relationship with Ross had been marvelous. How she'd loved lying in Ross's arms through the briskly cool fall nights, knowing that Adam was asleep in the next room, taking pleasure in the fact that they were a complete family again. She'd known ecstasy time and again when he'd turned toward her and gathered her into his arms, his lips claiming hers as she surrendered to him completely. Then all the differences between Ross and herself had paled in significance, and she'd felt deep in her heart that everything would work out.

With an effort, Diana blanked out the doubts that thinking about her mother and their conversation had raised again. She forced herself to scan the thick carpet for her earring.

"Darn!" she grumbled impatiently when she didn't see it. She dropped to her knees and spread her fingers into the thick pile to search for the back of her earring. But it seemed that it had vanished completely, absorbed into the carpet's depths as elusively as the proverbial needle in its haystack.

The sound of Ross's footsteps were likewise absorbed by the carpet as he strode down the hall to their bedroom.

"Hi, honey. I'm home," he called as he entered the room. His black-lashed, golden gaze swooped about the bedroom in puzzlement when his greeting was not immediately and cheerily returned, and for a moment he failed to see Diana on her knees behind the bed. He shrugged out of his jacket and slipped it onto a hanger.

"Hi…" she murmured absently at last without her usual enthusiasm, speaking like a seamstress with pins precariously balanced between pursed lips. She didn't even glance at him, so intent was she on the tiny bit of gold she was sifting into her fingers and carefully lifting from the floor.

He paused, leaning forward, observing her curious posture, thinking that her upturned derriere swathed in softly flowing black crepe looked very inviting. She really shouldn't get in that position if she wanted him to keep his hands off her, he thought with a smile. "The second honeymoon's over already, I see," he said, "and it's only been a month." The low rumbling sound of his chuckle followed his statement, its warmth a caress.

"Sorry, darling," she murmured absently, feeling guilt-stricken as she fastened the pearl securely at last to her earlobe. She caught the flash of amusement in his eyes and tried to smile. "I was looking for my earring when you came in. And dinner at mother's tonight—when she's just back from Europe fresh and relaxed and loaded for bear—her energy at such times for running my life is so enormous!'' At Ross's quick frown, her tone became pleading. ''You haven't talked to her, Ross....'' Diana's voice quavered. ''I feel as nervous as a cat.''

''You should scratch her then, and not me,'' he said abruptly.

''I did try to stand up to her, and she didn't like it.''

''I don't imagine that she would.'' Golden eyes stared at her thoughtfully, not liking the uncertainty he saw clouding her lovely face. Too often lately he'd seen the doubts she tried so hard to conceal. She always tried too damned hard at everything she did, and that included their reconciliation, he thought irritably. That was one of their problems, the way Diana worked at something fiercely when she was determined to succeed, a result of Madelaine's disciplined rearing.

Ross's eyes slid over his wife. How properly she had over-dressed for the evening, too perfectly. Still, if he knew Madelaine, she would find something to criticize. His lazy gaze swept Diana's figure-fitting black crepe gown, the single strand of pearls looped at her throat, the V neckline that revealed the contours of her shapely breasts. For once Diana's long black hair was secured in a severe, gleaming coil at the nape of her neck, a hairdo that she knew he didn't like because he thought it made her look too sophisticated and cold. Naturally the style was Madelaine's favorite.

"Mother was at her worst," Diana confided wearily, hoping to make him understand.

"I can imagine what she said," Ross said dryly, feeling genuinely annoyed at his mother-in-law's unfailing ability to interfere in their marriage and upset his wife.

"It might not have been so bad if she hadn't learned about our reconciliation from Hazel Epplebiele, of all people.... Mother was simply furious about that. She said that Hazel gloated unbearably when she realized that Mother didn't even know."

"Madelaine's anger has nothing to do with Hazel," Ross said roughly. "She's made no secret of the fact that she's never wanted us to get back together." Ross's movements were suddenly savage as he unthreaded his navy-maroon striped tie and tossed it onto the bed, no longer caring that such disorderliness goaded Diana. Then he ripped at the buttons of his pale blue shirt, exposing a strip of muscled teak-brown torso.

For a long moment Diana watched him, silently sympathizing with his anger, feeling guilty that she'd greeted him in such a negative way when he must be exhausted from a long day at the mill. "Ross...." Her low, gentle voice had gone husky as she moved toward him.

His dark scowl softened at the sight of her voluptuous body in motion, the soft crepe flowing over her every curve, the hem dancing lightly beneath her

knees. Tanned fingers fell away from the last button
on his shirt as her own hesitantly took their place.
Slowly she unfastened it for him in a wifely gesture
of affection. He saw a mixture of understanding and
compassion in her imploring, incandescent blue gaze
as well as the first hint of passion in their fiery depths.
Then she slid his shirt from his broad shoulders, her
hands tracing the smooth hard warmth of his flesh.
She was aware of him watching her, of his gold eyes
lighting with a burning intensity as they fastened on
the beauty of her face.

"I...didn't kiss you...when you came in...." she
murmured softly, stretching delicately onto her tiptoes
even as he bent his head to hers. Desperately she
wanted to banish all the lingering doubts her mother
had so deliberately raised about the ultimate success
of their relationship.

"I know...."

His lips seared hers with molten fire; rolling waves
of tingling flame radiated from where his mouth
touched hers. His arms slid around her waist, and he
pressed her tightly to him with a groan. She seemed
to melt against him, her flesh soft and yielding, utterly
feminine. He was aware of a fierce roar in his ears,
like that of an ocean's waves battering a desolate,
windswept beach.

For her, too, passion obliterated all else. His kiss
washed away the anxieties and frustrations she'd been
feeling only minutes before. For the moment, facing
Madelaine and her displeasure were forgotten. All her
doubts about Ross and their future were momentarily

pushed aside. Forgotten too was the strange fear that
had inexplicably seized Diana earlier that afternoon.
After she'd talked to her mother, Diana had gone outside, thinking physical work would be soothing to her
fragile nerves. She'd busied herself weeding her garden until it was time to pick Adam up from scouts.

A strange wind had whispered through the woods;
the moss had seemed to swing eerily from low cypress branches. It had seemed suddenly that despite
the bright sunlight, the trees had taken on dark, nightmarish shapes, that the normal forest sounds were terrifyingly monstrous. For a brief moment before fleeing inside in a frenzy of childish desperation and
locking all the doors behind her, Diana had been reminded of the strange dreams that had plagued her as
a child, of half-forgotten feelings that were all too
familiar. She had felt horribly alienated and lost, as
she had after she'd lost Tami, and it was only when
she had picked up Adam and brought him home again
that the terrible feelings had subsided. Had something
her mother said triggered her reaction in the forest?

Later she'd wondered if subconsciously her feelings about Tami had surfaced in this new and perplexing way, and she was determined that if she again
felt overwhelmed she would try not to run away. But
deep down she'd laughed at herself for thinking that
in the future she would be less cowardly, for wasn't
it easy to decide to be brave when the danger was
well past?

The sensation of lips branding her own with
scorching intensity brought Diana sharply into the

present. She reveled in the strong arms that wrapped her, in the solidness of Ross's hard chest beneath her head. She felt so utterly safe when he held her. His mouth was passionately raining kisses over her face, lightly touching her closed eyelids, her long black lashes, the pert tip of her nose, the winged darkness of a brow, as though every feature were precious to him. Her heart was pounding wildly at his caressing touches.

She felt his fingers in her hair. A shower of black pins pelted the soft carpet, and her hair cascaded through his hands, tumbling in gleaming waves down her back.

"Ross," she murmured faintly in protest, "that hairdo took me nearly thirty minutes..."

"Don't waste your time like that again then, honey," he murmured, chuckling, "when you know I like it much better this way." He nibbled at her earlobe, and then sent a shivering trail of fire along her throat as he explored the sensitive, pale flesh with his lips.

She was aware of the zipper ripping, of the black dress sliding away, of the heat of him as he drew her down onto the soft carpet.

"Ross...."

"I know...it took you an hour to dress...." he mumbled distractedly, his mouth lowering once again to explore the hollow between her breasts with such ravaging expertise that Diana was a churning mass of desire.

"No," she murmured faintly. "We need a towel...."

"What?"

"We need..."

Suddenly she was aware of him trembling, of a deep masculine rumble of sound as his warm, rich laughter filled the room. At last his sensual lips curved into a broad grin as he choked back his last chuckle. "Good Lord, Diana! That would be a killing remark to a normal, frail male ego. Fortunately mine is abnormally healthy, substantial enough to withstand a little battering," he finished wryly.

With her fingertip she fondly traced the edge of his mouth. "I'm sorry, Ross," she said softly. "I didn't mean...to hurt your feelings."

"I thought I'd swept you off your feet—literally."

"I am on the floor," she chuckled. "Why don't I give you a second chance to redeem yourself and bolster that insufferable ego of yours?" she murmured huskily against his mouth, savoring the deliciously heady sensation of his nearness as she arched her body, shaping herself to him.

Tenderly he pushed back a wayward tendril of her raven hair. "My tidy wanton," he murmured before his lips closed gently over hers, his kiss deepening even as their need for each other grew into an all-consuming urgency.

Diana felt warmly aglow as she stepped from the bathtub, sudsy froth clinging to her golden shoulders as she toweled herself dry. She felt so wonderful, she didn't even care if they were late to her mother's tonight. With a smile she saw her black dress in a tangled heap on the floor where they'd made love, and she hoped that it wasn't too wrinkled to wear. Ross had already showered, dressed and gone downstairs to find Adam and make sure he was ready to go.

Her damp feet scurried noiselessly across the thick carpet of her bedroom. Glancing at Ross's alarm clock out of the corner of her eye and seeing the lateness of the hour, she flew about the room, gathering up her dress and lingerie with one motion of her wrist, swiftly brushing her hair in four strokes, dabbing on a trace of powder, misting a dash of cologne in her hair. They would just make it on time if she hurried, she thought as she did a little shimmy and wriggled provocatively into her black dress, kicking her black strapless heels into position and sliding her stockinged feet into them.

In less than five minutes she was breathlessly roping her pearls over her neck with one hand and scooping up her black clutch handbag with the other as she walked out of the bedroom door into the hall.

She didn't look the same as she had before Ross had made love to her, and she realized uneasily that Madelaine's sharp eyes would probably note every incriminating detail. Gone was her careful composure, her demure restraint. The wild, passionate side of her nature was poorly concealed. Her makeup was a little blurred about her eyes, eyes which seemed all soft sparkle and yielding allure. Her gentle smile was drowsily voluptuous, her cheeks flushed. In agitation she tried to smooth her hair, which tumbled down her back in the gleaming, satiny mass that Ross preferred. But the gesture was ineffectual.

She felt giddy and lightheaded, like a seventeen-year-old in love, and she'd been married to the same man for years. She could hear Ross and Adam downstairs in the den talking as they waited for her.

When she reached the landing, she leaned over the railing to call down a gay greeting. But her words clogged in her throat, which had suddenly gone dry; her smile froze into a silly little crumpled line when she caught the sense of their conspiratorial conversation. In an incautious moment Adam's enthusiastic voice had risen, his words drifting all too clearly in the silent house to her ears. Her fingers tightened even more painfully on the rail when she caught the deep resonance of Ross's deliberately hushed tone.

"Don't speak so loudly, son. I don't want to upset your mother with this just yet."

Diana's cheeks paled as a cold white rage went through her; her blood seemed to turn to ice in her veins. Yet some violent force still pumped her heart. But despite her fury, a team of harnessed stallions couldn't have dragged her away. Deliberately she backed out of the light so that she was completely hidden from them.

More than once Adam and Ross had teamed up on her, making plans without asking her during the two days every week she was away in Houston. Once Ross gave his permission to Adam, he could rarely be persuaded, no matter how hard she tried, to change his mind.

"You mean you'll let me take your sleeping bag and all your gear on the canoe trip this weekend?" Adam continued.

"As long as you promise to take care of it the way I taught you...."

"What about Mother?" Adam queried doubtfully.

"Leave your mother to me."

That last was too much! Diana felt explosive as she rushed breathlessly down the steps, her white face and tight lips instantly revealing to Ross that she'd overheard enough of their conversation to guess the rest.

"What canoe trip?" she hurled.

"This weekend the scouts..." Ross began before she cut him off.

"This weekend! Do you mean Friday, three days from now?"

"That's right," Ross admitted. "Friday and Saturday night Adam's troop is planning a camping and canoeing trip. I thought it would be a great experience for him."

"Are you going?"

"No, but two other fathers and the scoutmaster are."

Ross rose slowly from the couch and strode to Diana. She saw kindness and compassion in his eyes. "I wanted to discuss this with you," he began.

"Obviously," she snapped sarcastically.

"But these discussions are always so fraught with

your unreasoning fear and hostility that I kept putting it off,'' he said gently, his steady gaze holding hers.

Somewhere in her mind she registered that she wasn't the only one who'd been trying to avoid fights this past month. But she was too furious to think logically, too caught up in the justice of her own point of view to consider his.

"Do you blame me for being afraid something might happen? Tami…''

"You felt this way even before Tami, and I've never understood why,'' he continued reasonably. "Children aren't hothouse plants. They have to have certain freedoms and independent experiences to develop normally. You can't possibly guard their every move without doing far more harm than good.''

"That's your opinion!'' Her voice was waspish and hot, but she didn't care.

"Yes, it is,'' he said coldly. "And Adam is *my* son. He's going on that canoe trip whether you like it or not.''

"End of discussion! Right?'' she jeered humorlessly, the pain she felt nearly overwhelming her. Rarely did he throw up the fact that he was Adam's biological parent while she was not, but always when he did so it hurt.

She was aware of Adam, paralyzed on the couch, his small face blanched, his mouth pinched as he listened to his parents argue about him. Suddenly she remembered how terrible she'd felt as a child when she'd been the cause of disagreements between her parents, and she realized how much worse this must be for Adam because of their recent separation. With an effort she tried to tone down her agitation.

"Diana, I would give anything if we could agree about this," Ross said on an apologetic note, though she knew there wasn't the slightest chance of relenting. What he wanted was for her to agree with him.

She was stiff as a piece of wood as his arms slid around her. His lips lightly brushed her forehead in a tender kiss. "I wish there was something I could do or say to make you feel less anxious. Adam will be okay. He has to learn to be on his own. Please try to understand."

She was trying, but she couldn't. A horrible vision that was somehow familiar rose up in her mind. Adam was helplessly alone and lost in a dark forest. Because of her terror she gripped Ross's hands tightly, holding on to him in a vain effort to banish her fears.

She didn't blame him for thinking her silly and ridiculous. He was so strong; she wondered if such a man could know the meaning of fear.

"There is something, Ross," she said quietly at last, "that would make me feel less anxious."

"What?" he asked gently. She was aware of his warm fingers soothingly caressing away the tension at the base of her neck, of his other hand clasping her firmly at the back of the waist.

"Please...don't plan these things behind my back. It will only make me more nervous if I think you're hiding something like this. I'd rather know...." She laid her head against the solid warmth of his chest.

"All right," he agreed. "I'll admit that was damned unfair of me."

He held her for a long time, but that glorious afterglow she'd experienced after he'd made love to her earlier was gone, and she was more painfully aware than ever of the gaping problems that existed between them. Not for the first time she wondered if two people as different as they were could ever make it.

When Madelaine opened the front door of her pretentious, redbrick mansion herself, her smile was so stiff and bright it looked as if she'd painted it on with the rest of her makeup. Diana cringed inwardly as her mother's china-blue gaze swept her briefly, feeling fortunate when it settled on Adam.

As always when confronted with her mother after a long absence, Diana was vaguely shocked to discover that her mother wasn't a giant of vast proportions, for over the phone she had the commanding personality of a much larger woman. With the passing of time she grew in Diana's imagination like Alice sprouting in her Wonderland. Silently Diana wondered how this tiny person could have represented such a powerful force in her life. But for all her lack of size, her mother had the will of a battleship commander, a will all the more formidable because she lacked a battleship to command.

In stiletto heels Madelaine measured scarcely five feet three inches, but her silvered hair was feathered to help achieve the illusion of height, just as her clothes were skillfully tailored to make her appear

taller. She was artfully groomed in pale blue silk that
matched her eyes, her full-breasted figure as perfect
as it had been on her wedding day, a boast she sometimes made to plump Hazel Epplebiele when she
found her best friend's gloating conceits about her
four brilliant children unendurable and desired to take
her down a notch. To keep herself so trim Madelaine
maintained a rigid schedule of exercises, spent four
weeks a year at expensive spas and adhered to a
grueling diet. Despite her size, she was a woman of
massive energy, throwing herself into everything that
she did from running charity bazaars to running her
daughter's life with a total and zealous dedication.

Even though Madelaine had been in Europe five
weeks, she didn't take either Diana or Adam in her
arms. Not because she didn't love them, but because
it simply wasn't her way.

"Adam, you may go into the playroom," Madelaine said, speaking in the same formal tone she might
have used from the podium when addressing a charity
league luncheon. "Ella Lou put all the things I
brought you from Europe on the toy chest."

Adam brightened at once. His grandmother kept up
with his interests and always bought marvelous pres-
ents, frequently things his parents would never have
allowed him to have. He remembered to restrain himself and said very politely, "Thank you, Grandmother." Madelaine beamed benignly, so genuinely
pleased that she almost smiled. With that Adam made
a beeline toward the playroom, starting to run when

he rounded the corner and thought he was safely out of his grandmother's sight.

But Madelaine, who had ears like an elephant, heard his quickened steps falling lightly on the glossily waxed, blond oak flooring before he reached the runner of thick blue carpet at the foot of the winding staircase. "Don't run inside, Adam dear," she called sharply after him, but by then he was safely away and had every intention of doing exactly as he pleased.

Without Adam as a buffer, Diana felt completely exposed to her mother's critical gaze, which kept returning to her mane of untidily cascading hair. Defiantly she tossed her head and placed her arm through Ross's.

Madelaine seemed to see her son-in-law for the first time, and she frowned slightly. Only to appear cordial she spoke to him in dismissal. "Ross, Richard is in the den."

Ross smiled down at his mother-in-law, but his smile was guarded and didn't crinkle the tanned skin beneath his eyes. He had not missed the lack of greeting, nor the lack of warmth in her voice. Deliberately he ignored her command that he leave.

"I'd like to see Father, too," Diana inserted, aware that her voice seemed to ring desperately throughout the vast high-ceilinged house, as it had always done when she was a child.

Madelaine's eyes glazed. "Of course, dear, but if you wouldn't mind, come into the kitchen in a few minutes. Patricia and I need a little help."

Madelaine was ushering them through the house

she was so proud of, beneath the soaring drama of a redwood-planked ceiling, rough-hewn fir beams, beneath the elegant counterpoint of a bronzed chandelier, its crystal fragments as coldly aglitter as blades of ice. They stepped deeply upon the softness of heirloom Oriental rugs and passed through innumerable elegant rooms stuffed with antique French furniture, too formal in style to be sat upon comfortably. Many of the pieces were priceless; Madelaine had spent a lifetime studiously acquiring them at auctions and in Europe.

But for all its beauty, Diana always dreaded spending time in her mother's home. Perhaps this was partially because every item in the house had been carefully selected to intimidate. The house had the look-don't-touch feel of a museum, and as usual, no matter the season, there was a distinct chill in the air. Diana shivered involuntarily, and though the house had once been her home, she realized anew how uncomfortable she'd always been in it, how acutely she'd felt that she didn't belong. Perhaps she had gone into design because of a deep need to fashion homes people *wanted* to live in and enjoy.

"I didn't realize Aunt Patricia was here," Diana said, making idle conversation.

Patricia, who was Madelaine's younger sister, was a pediatrician living in Denver. She had never married.

"You know Patricia went to Europe with us?" Madelaine was saying. Diana nodded. "Well, Richard finally talked her into selling her property adjacent to his office, and she came home with us to negotiate the sale. She's being rather difficult, I'm afraid. But then you know how she is.''

They stepped into the den and her father greeted Diana and Ross warmly, heartily shaking Ross's hand and then squeezing his daughter into his arms against his rotund belly in a tight bear hug. Only an inch taller than his wife when she wore heels, Richard was a fat little man too comfortable with himself to diet as religiously as Madelaine would have wished, though on occasion he could show unusual willpower and refrain from the second slice of his favorite cheesecake. But Madelaine adored him despite his imperfections and lack of discipline, liking him perhaps all the more because of them. With her husband, and only with him, Madelaine was soft, even enduring his demonstrative affection in public, blushing with pleasure like a girl at times. Theirs had been a love match, and their passion had deepened with the passing of years.

Madelaine left them to visit while she saw about dinner. Diana stayed with the men as long as she possibly could, but when the clock on the mantel chimed the quarter hour for the second time, she hastily excused herself, remembering her promise to her mother.

The delicious scents of braised beef tips and sautéed mushrooms wafted in the air. When Diana entered the kitchen, Patricia was unfortunately nowhere to be seen, having gone to the study to take a private telephone call from the current man in her life. As they worked together, the atmosphere between mother and daughter was heavy.

"I do hope that you don't mind my saying this, Diana," Madelaine began at last in the over-solicitous manner that grated on Diana's nerves, "but don't you think you would look much better with your hair up instead of in that fly-away style that makes you look like one of those wild hippie types?"

Diana set the crystal salad dishes down with a clatter. "Ross likes it this way, Mother."

"And is he the reason you're as pale as chalk? If you were to ask me, you don't look happy at all!"

"I'm not asking, Mother."

Louvered doors swung wildly, as if a rowdy gunslinger had barged inside a saloon.

"Diana," Aunt Patricia shrieked in a voice so distinctively her own that once it was heard, it was always remembered. She'd never lost, as Madelaine had quite deliberately, the North Texas nasal twang of her childhood. She bounded into the kitchen with her customary exuberance, unwittingly interrupting the uncomfortable exchange between mother and daughter. Plump, spoiled Sylvie turned into a haired ball of fire and spat furiously from the barstool where she'd been napping as Patricia sailed by her; Sylvie, who was seventeen and quite old for a cat, was accustomed to the normally tomblike silence of the vast house and couldn't tolerate sudden noises or people rushing about her in an incomprehensible flurry of excitement.

Madelaine looked up with irritation from the thickening hollandaise sauce she was stirring, observing her sister through eyes that had narrowed like her cat's. Sylvie, too, was watching Patricia suspiciously, her ears flattened against her orange head, the tip of her fluffy tail flicking as she resettled herself

Patricia, however, had the air of one deliberately oblivious to the undercurrents in the room. In the first place she despised cats, for once, in her childhood, she'd teased the wrong cat and been viciously scratched. In the second place she still enjoyed the rebelliousness of her younger-sister role even though she was well past fifty. Besides, having learned long ago that Madelaine had a rule for absolutely everything under the sun, she'd decided at the age of three that it was best to ignore them all, and did exactly as she pleased when in her company or anyone else's for that matter, though she could at times appear to be dutiful about listening to her older sister's lectures. But that was only when she was very weary and could think of nothing better to do.

Though Patricia was a carbon copy or rather a blond copy of her older sister in physical appearance, and though she had the same formidable amount of energy, there all resemblance ended. Patricia was a free spirit, spontaneous and unorthodox, totally unpredictable and thereby completely exasperating to the disciplined Madelaine. But, as if frequently the case between two such opposites in temperament, they adored each other, each tolerating and understanding the other in some deep and basic way. They even relished, though neither would have admitted it for the world, the hot disagreements that could erupt so easily between them.

Patricia's total admiring concentration was fixed on her tall, slim niece. She had clasped both of Diana's hands in her own forceful grip and was eyeing her in that swift, nervously intent way of hers that made Diana feel she was having her bone marrow examined. As always when Patricia was motionless for a second, there was a feeling of suspended animation about her. She was like a tightly coiled human spring, quiet and still only between bounces.

"I think it's wonderful that you and Ross have gotten back together! Absolutely wonderful!"

A spoon began to clank furiously against the pot that was being stirred.

"Thank you, Aunt Patricia. I'm terribly happy about it myself." Diana was smiling gently, her beautiful face illuminated.

"I never did understand why you two separated, but that's in the past now.... If only I could have met someone like him myself...years ago...." she said dreamily. "Who knows? I might have married and padded about as comfortably entrenched in that well-worn rut of respectability as Madelaine has all these years."

Madelaine shot her a killing look that Patricia chose not to see, for that subject was a sore point between them.

Though Patricia had remained single, men and their love were not commodities she'd chosen to live without, and she'd had a long string of relationships with a fascinating assortment of men, a way of life Madelaine heartily disapproved of. Once, years ago, when Madelaine had voiced an objection to an Argentinian shipping magnate Patricia had been seeing, Patricia had responded in her emphatic way, "Then I certainly won't marry him, Madelaine dear. He has asked me, you know…and I was considering it, but it would never do to bring a man into the family if you didn't like him. I shall simply have to keep looking…."

Patricia had kept looking for twenty years, and on the few occasions when Madelaine had dared to voice the opinion that Patricia should settle down and live respectably with a husband, Patricia would reply in that infuriatingly breezy manner of hers, "Well, no man has ever suited me as Rafael did, dear, and you didn't like him. I would be married now—if you hadn't objected." This reply was a painful cross in Madelaine's life, that it should have been she, who most wanted her sister properly married, who had prevented it.

The atmosphere in the kitchen was growing unbearably heavy.

"You know, dear," Patricia continued to Diana, "that I've always liked Ross immensely."

"Patricia," Madelaine snapped, the spoon clattering ominously. "You don't really know Ross, or you wouldn't say that. He drove Diana away with his high-handed tactics."

"Our separation was my fault and not Ross's, Mother, as I've told you scores of times."

"Without any further explanation, I might add," Madelaine said huffily, her nose thrust high into the air.

"There were private reasons," Diana said quietly, her experience this afternoon in the forest enabling her to recall too vividly the numbed, emotional turmoil that had driven the final wedge between herself and Ross.

"You're protecting Ross when you say that," Madelaine insisted. "I've always known he did something so terrible to you that you couldn't bring yourself to confide it."

"That's not it, Mother," Diana began desperately. "But I can't tell you everything about my marriage...or even explain everything about myself. I'm not a child any longer, and I can't run to my mother with all my problems."

Patricia could contain herself no longer. She was fairly bursting to speak. "Madelaine, as a doctor I always advise the parents of my patients not to push too hard for confidences, that it only makes them more difficult to obtain."

Madelaine's quick glance toward her sister was smoldering. "I hate to say this, Patricia dear," Madelaine returned in that particularly sour-sweet tone of hers that was a warning to close friends to beware, "but you're a pediatrician and not a psychiatrist."

"I don't have to be a psychiatrist to know meddling when I see it, Madelaine," Patricia said, "and I see it right now."

"Oooooh!" Madelaine sucked in a long, furious

breath. Patricia, who was one of the few people who dared to so outrageously cross her, had pushed her to the limits of her somewhat limited patience. Still, her voice was as falsely sweet as a sugar substitute. "You'd have to be a mother yourself to understand what it's like for me to…see Diana back with that man. I want her to be happy, and she's never been happy a day in her life with him! If you only had a child of your own, you might have some shred of maternal understanding! But you never had a baby yourself…like I did."

Madelaine stopped suddenly, appalled at herself. The color had drained alarmingly from her face, and for a minute Diana was afraid she might collapse. Her expression was so odd; Diana had never seen it before.

To Diana's amazement, for once Patricia was quite as speechless as her older sister. There seemed to be something unsaid between them, something that was terribly important, like a long-guarded secret. Strangely neither of them had the courage to look at Diana. For the first time in her life Diana saw fear in her mother's eyes, a crack in her normally stout emotional armor. For an instant she looked quite old and fragile, and Diana felt strangely tender and protective toward her.

Patricia's expression was also unmistakably strange, and for the briefest moment Diana saw a deep, inexplicable compassion there. Then the little awkwardness between them passed, with both sisters speaking hastily at once, as if to cover their lapse. Yet it was there, as uncomfortable as an uninvited dinner guest, for the rest of the evening.

Madelaine's dinner party passed as Madelaine's dinner parties usually passed, with the sexes being divided except for the duration of the dinner. Patricia was lively and entertaining, changing topics of conversation quickly before they could be explored too deeply, for she was too easily bored to do otherwise. And perhaps she'd learned her lesson earlier in the evening. Tonight she seemed especially bright, deliberately and distractingly so.

Much to Diana's relief, not once did either Madelaine or Patricia bring up the subject of Ross or Diana's marriage again. But Diana was, nevertheless, aware of an uneasiness that had lingered between the two sisters ever since Madelaine's outburst. Again Diana had the impression that they had somehow blundered into territory that long ago they had forbidden themselves.

Once, when Diana came unexpectedly into the kitchen with a stack of dessert dishes, she caught a single phrase from her mother and aunt's hushed conversation.

"You really should have told her years ago, Madelaine...."

Then, seeing her, both women fell awkwardly silent when Diana entered, and Diana had the uncomfortable feeling they had been talking about her. Again the little awkwardness was brushed over, and this time Diana was too upset by her own problems, which she had been dwelling on, to think about it.

Throughout the evening she'd found it increasingly difficult to concentrate on the thread of Aunt Patricia's lively chatter. Her thoughts kept returning to Ross and Adam, and she felt strangely alienated from them. It was as though she were no longer sure she could fit herself back into their lives. For three years they'd survived without her. Perhaps they would be better off if she gave up. Ever since her argument with Ross earlier in the evening the belief had begun to grow that Ross and Adam waited eagerly for every Wednesday, when she would leave for Houston for two days, that they used this time to make plans she couldn't approve of. She didn't like the nagging feeling that she was making the two people she loved more than anyone else in the world so unhappy.

What was the matter with her? Was she so like her mother that she couldn't allow her own child the freedom he needed to live normally?

That night when she and Ross were home in bed he reached for her, pulling her shaking body into the comforting strength of his hard arms. Ross felt her stiffen when he touched her, but gradually the heat of him melted Diana against his length.

His breath was like a feather's caress against her throat when he said very gently, "You were awfully quiet all evening."

"Sorry." Her single choked word didn't sound much like an apology.

"Are you still upset about Adam going camping?" She was aware of his fingers stroking her bare shoulder in a circular motion with languorous slowness, the touch of him pleasantly warm.

"I suppose that's part of it," she admitted, her fear in her voice.

"Well, maybe I was unfair to give my permission without asking you first. I'll find an excuse to keep him home—this time," Ross said at last. "He'll be disappointed, but..." Idly his hand brushed her hair from her forehead, as though she were a child he sought to comfort.

"No!" The word seemed to be jerked painfully from her.

"What?"

"Don't you see, Ross, I'd be a monster in his eyes. Whatever reason you gave him, he'd know the real one—that I don't want him to go."

A roughened finger tilted her chin upward, forcing her to look at him. He stared so deeply into her eyes that her heart tripped at a faster pace at the gentleness of the expression on his craggy, masculine face. "You wouldn't ever be a monster in his eyes," he said softly. "Adam understands how you feel. But you're right, of course—he would be very disappointed."

His finger moved to explore the soft lines of her face, touching her lips to trace their shape. His hand moved so expertly, so lightly across the sensitive softness of her mouth, that her lips parted, inviting a finger inside. Sexily she nibbled at it with her teeth and warm tongue.

"And I don't want that," she said breathlessly, beginning to lose the thread of their conversation. "I want him to be happy."

He continued to move his finger inside her mouth. Suddenly it was very difficult for her to breathe evenly. There was an erotic element in what he was doing, something that stimulated every sense in her body, especially since his gaze was watching her steadily, absorbing every detail of the delicate movement of her mouth on his finger with disturbing interest.

He removed his hand slowly as though with reluctance. "And I want you to be happy," Ross said, the deep resonance of his voice wrapping her with his love.

"I am happy, Ross...." Her voice broke, and she was grateful for that first velvet softness of his lips touching hers before his kiss hardened, his tongue seeking out hers, and she was no longer expected to speak.

Diana wanted to be happy so desperately, but suddenly that simple desire seemed so frustratingly elusive and impossible. She was almost glad that tomorrow was Wednesday and she would be going to Houston. Suddenly she was afraid, more afraid than she'd ever been in her life; she was sure that she was losing Ross and Adam, as surely as she'd lost them three years ago.

Like a condemned man with one last wish before the inevitable end, Diana wanted Ross more than ever before that night. She surrendered with total abandon to the demand of the ravishing lips brutally taking

hers in an ever-deepening kiss, to the roughly caressing hands moving over her body with savage urgency,
to the heat of a passion so hot and wild that it consumed them in a burning inferno all their own.

He took her, loving her with shattering forceful
passion. In that last shuddering moment, he was overwhelmed with feelings of incomprehensible intensity,
of his overpowering love for her, of fulfillment and
deep contentment, of blazing emotions so wildly pleasurable that they were beyond all his past experiences.

When his breathing stilled, and she knew he was
asleep, she drew away into herself, curling her body
into a tight ball of pain as hot tears overflowed her
eyes and ran like scalding acid down her cheeks. His
lovemaking had been like a precious treasure, all the
more precious because her time with him was so terribly threatened.

She would lose him—irrevocably—for she didn't
seem capable of changing that part of herself that was
driving them apart.

It was only a question of when.

The dining room was softly aglow in candlelight, the table romantically set for two. This morning when Ross had kissed her before he left for work, he'd whispered that he wanted this weekend to be for them alone, a kind of honeymoon. So she had busied herself to keep from thinking, cooking a roast marinated in delicate spices, dirty rice, Ross's favorite Cajun dish, as well as crawfish gumbo. She'd tossed his favorite spinach salad, which was now chilling in the refrigerator, and now that everything was done, a terrifying restlessness stirred through her.

As she moved about the room arranging everything, her tall, lithe figure was infinitely graceful, her every gesture exquisitely feminine, and always everything that she did lent beauty to her surroundings, just as she herself was beautiful. She was braless in a caftan of shimmering emerald velour, and the top three buttons were provocatively parted to reveal the tantalizing swell of softly voluptuous décolletage. The rich jewel color enhanced against her dark beauty, brightening her blue eyes, contrasting against her too-pale skin and ruby-red lips; the gold rope at her tiny waist showed off the allure of her slimness above the swaying curve of well-turned hips and slender thighs.

She wanted to please Ross so much, but in spite of all her efforts to be calm she felt very tense about Adam. She knew that Ross deeply disapproved of what he called her overprotectiveness where Adam was concerned. But Adam was out there...alone in the forest. She cast a furtive glance toward the window, and then forced her gaze away as she heard

Ross's low wolf whistle as he stepped into the dining room, his golden eyes alight with masculine admiration, while at the same time he scanned her face intently, reading her every emotion. His dark handsomeness was rakishly mesmerizing, and she drew in a quick, sharp breath at the sight of him leaning negligently, looking boldly handsome, in the doorway. She fought back the desire to throw herself into his arms and confide her terror; she knew it would only anger him. He wanted her to be thinking of him and not worrying about Adam. But she'd never been very good at concealing her feelings from him. The line of his lips hardened slightly when he saw her fear and guessed the reason behind it, but his avid gaze, lingering where jeweled fabric stretched across the fullness of her breasts, remained hot with male interest.

She flushed warmly, awash in tremulous sensation, as a terrifyingly pleasurable current ran through her body. His mere glance evoked an acute physical longing.

He stepped into the room, and moving toward her, folded her gently into his arms. He was like a tall broad-shouldered giant, as lean and latently powerful as a jungle animal, and something that was primitive and carnal drew her to him. Her eyes were shining when she looked up at him, but he remained, despite her attempt to pretend she was happy, uneasily aware of her agitation about Adam, of the fear she was fighting. Letting his desire rule him, he fought back his own feelings of simmering anger; he thought he was unfair in not trying to understand her feelings about Adam.

With surprising gentleness he placed both his hands on each side of her face. "You're very beautiful tonight," he said. His low voice was a husky caress flowing over her body. He lifted aside a thick length of raven hair and his hard mouth dusted her sensitive flesh with tortuously erotic feelings. He knew how to kiss a woman and make her feel totally feminine. His warm breath fanned her creamy skin; his lips and tongue nuzzled her intimately in a leisurely fashion, as though he had the whole night to make her his. Desire tingled in her arteries, and an all-pervading weakness made her go limp in his arms.

"Don't," she pleaded faintly as Ross lifted his mouth from her skin and began boldly unfastening the remaining buttons on her bodice so that his hands could slide inside and cup the soft fullness of her breasts.

"Why not?" he whispered, his voice pitched low and husky as he undid the last button, loosening the gown so that its velvet texture eased downward over her bare skin. "You want this as much as I do."

"There's...dinner. I cooked all afternoon."

"Honey, why do you always spend so much time on the wrong things?" he said, chuckling, before he lowered his head to let his mouth slide down her throat to tease her breasts with ardent, feather-light kisses. Her nipples grew hard in his mouth as he nibbled first one and then the other, pressing his head between the ample curving mounds, letting his lips ravish her slowly in sensual exploration. With her eyes tightly shut, she felt the warmth of his mouth stroking erogenous places, teasing her with his expert, titillating love play.

"I...I thought you wanted me to cook," she replied breathlessly, arching her body against his. "You said we'd stay home...."

He laughed, savoring the feel of her. The warm masculine sound of him filled her with radiating pleasure. His mouth stopped the sexual conquest of her ripe, voluptuous breasts and lingeringly traveled upward to her half-parted lips. In the air-conditioning her damp, exposed and very feminine flesh felt cool without his hot mouth covering her until the warm globes were unmercifully crushed against the fiery granite of his chest. "I wasn't thinking about cooking...when I said that," he muttered fiercely. Then he began to kiss her throat, pausing to smooth aside a tumbling lock of black hair from her face. Very slowly he brought her face up to his, seeking the rosy, pouting fruit of those delicately swollen lips that so tempted him. God...she could drive a man crazy....

Dinner was forgotten, both of them utterly lost in a tempestuous sea of whirling passions. Time and place were forgotten; each was aware only of the other. With black-lashed eyes still shut, she surrendered to the virile, masculine man who held her so tightly, whose hard, sensual mouth claimed hers with a tenderly bruising force. She surrendered with the utter totality of that wild, untamed side of her nature

to the wanton desires that coursed like fire through
her body.

Her hands moved over him, giving him pleasure
with their touch. She undressed him, unfastening
every button on his shirt with tantalizing slowness
before she unsnapped his slacks, drawing them downward over taut thighs. The hard male strength of him
made her feverishly aware that his desire was as great
as hers, and she lay still as he fitted his body to hers,
positioning her beneath him, his thigh resting intimately between her softly enveloping warmth.

"Ross." His name was a moan of pleasure before
his lips sought the source of the sound.

Her arms crept about his neck and shoulders, feeling the hardened, flexed muscles of his back beneath
her fingers.

A low rumble vibrated through the house; outside
lightning flashed, lighting the darkening sky. Instantly
the passion flowed out of her. It was like an arctic
wind throwing the door of a warm room open and all
the heat going out in a rush.

In a dreamlike daze she pushed him away. Her
heart throbbed painfully; her breathing was ragged.
But her eyes, darting frantically toward the window,
were filled with fear. She would have stumbled immediately toward the window had Ross not been
holding her so tightly against himself that escape was
impossible.

"Damn!" he cursed, his low voice calling her fear-
filled gaze back to him. Anger and impatience blazed
in his flaming eyes. "What the hell..."

"Adam..." she choked, "is out there."

"I know that." Ross's low tone was strangely tight, his fury and frustration with her barely leashed. "That's no reason..."

"I can't help it, Ross."

For over a month he'd held tight rein on his feelings concerning the way she tried to smother Adam. He'd tried to fathom the reasons that lay behind what he could only consider her irrational fears, but her terror tonight was the last straw.

Her large, luminous blue eyes implored him to understand, but he was past understanding as he grabbed his slacks from the floor and stepped into them. She stood very still and frightened, watching him, a strange numbness invading her emotions, cutting her off from him.

The hell he was going to let her baby Adam until his son was as cowardly as she was. He stared at her face, which was filled with blank despair, and his anger intensified.

He knew that particular look on her face too well. It was the one expression that could re-open all the old wounds that had led to their separation. She was coldly remote, as though she were a statue hewn of stone. That's how she'd been after Tami had died. He stuffed his shirt inside his waistband without bothering to button it all the way up so that a strip of teak-brown torso was revealed.

"Well." He looked up at her, his own expression rough and utterly lacking in sympathy because of his own pain, his eyes smoldering. "Are you going to stand there all night and taunt me with what I can't have?''

She trembled as she grew aware of the heat in his male eyes hungrily devouring her pale golden flesh before she stooped gracefully and retrieved her voluminous velour gown and pulled it on. He stared at her hard, observing her every fumbling movement as she dressed. When she had trouble with the buttons of her bodice, he dragged her into his arms, his fingers yanking them together as he buttoned them all the way up to her neck.

She cringed at his warm touch, at the savagery that drove him, welcoming the moment when he released her and pushed her away from him. Vaguely she was conscious of a new coldness in him, too, that all-too-familiar unrelenting hardness, and she was reminded of the way he'd been when he'd thrown her out three years before. She knew she was pushing him, but she couldn't stop herself.

''I might as well eat,'' he said, leaving her, ''while you cower.''

She flinched but said nothing as he stalked from the room. She heard the sound of cabinet doors being slammed, of lids and pots smashing together as he served himself supper. He didn't return to the dining room, preferring to remain in the kitchen to avoid her company.

She didn't dare join him. Besides, her concern toward him was nothing compared to the tormenting fear she had about Adam. Nothing seemed to matter any longer, not even Ross. There was only her fear, and he was the cause. She pushed that last into the background of her mind.

A thunderclap resounded, shaking the entire house this time. She tore across the room and thrust the drapes aside, pushing her white face against the cool glass as she stared out into the sultry thickness of the darkness. Raindrops began to pelt downward, sliding against the window panes until she couldn't see anything through the slithering droplets, but she stood there transfixed with terror.

Hours passed, but she was not aware of time or of her own exhaustion. Once when Ross came into the room, probably with the intention of apologizing, she deliberately ignored him. What was there after all that she could say when he refused even to try to understand her torment? What did she care for the haunted pain she saw in his eyes when Adam was out there in the violence of that storm?

Shortly before midnight the telephone rang, its bleated bursts of sound as shatteringly turbulent as the storm outside.

Diana rushed toward it just as Ross's steady, tanned hand lifted the receiver from the hook. She was instantly electrified with fear by something in Ross's tone.

"He's what?" Ross asked, and fear jerked through her like a whiplash.

Her own anxiety was so overwhelming that she couldn't concentrate on what Ross was saying. The sense of it came to her in a blur of sound, like nightmarish fragments in a dream, fitting together into a pattern of horror.

Adam and the scout he'd been partners with in a canoe were missing. They'd been racing the other kids and had canoed past the spot where they should have gotten out. The others had been searching for hours. Adam's overturned canoe had been found snagged against a tree stump, two orange life preservers floating nearby.

If they were alive, Adam and the other child were missing in the forest. Every feeling in Diana's heart seemed to freeze, her emotional lifeblood seeping out of her like blood flowing from a gaping wound. When Ross reached her, his own face white with pain and compassion for her suffering, she drew away, shutting him out. For an instant he looked stupefied with his own agony, as though in the deepest recesses of his heart he couldn't really comprehend her turning from him. But then with remembered pain he did understand.

His features hardened, and he gazed at her with a fierce determination that at any time would have chilled her. He looked exactly as he had the night he'd thrown her out, but she didn't care. She couldn't imagine that she'd ever want him again. He'd sent Adam out there! Though this time she didn't say it, she blamed him as much as she had before. Despite her silence, he saw it in her face. He heard the horrible, unspoken accusation in his mind as clearly as if she'd shouted it a thousand times.

"I want you to promise me that you'll call your

aunt Patricia," he began very coldly, "and have her come over here so you won't be alone."

"Okay," she managed in a barely audible whisper, "but...why?"

"I'm going out—to find Adam." He was jerking on a bright yellow slicker and stepping into thick knee-high rubber boots he frequently used at work when he had to go out into the forest. "You can quit looking at me like I'm some kind of monster! I didn't kill our child! Not Tami! And not Adam!" He grabbed an enormous silver floodlight out of a drawer. "He's all right, damn you!" he muttered furiously. "He has to be... But you and I..." He paused, staring long and hard at the frozen beauty of her face as if to measure his words. "You and I are finished. I should have realized that a long time ago. I can't live with a woman who becomes a zombie every time our child walks out the front door and then points her finger at me if the slightest thing goes wrong. That's a guilt trip I won't handle."

So, it was over...as it had been before, she thought dully. She'd killed their love by making the same mistake a second time, but in her mood of gripping despair she couldn't even care, she thought as she watched his retreating form vanish into the darkness. Even though she knew that when she got past this pressing pain his leaving her would thrust her into a lifetime of loneliness and agony, she could feel nothing as she watched him disappear into the thickly falling curtain of rain.

* * *

Aunt Patricia bounced through the front door almost immediately after Diana called her, and she seemed as vivaciously bright at one in the morning as she always was in the middle of the day. Perhaps it went with her profession and the fact that she was used to calls in the middle of the night.

"Not to worry, love!" Aunt Patricia advised cheerily, masking her deep and immediate concern at the sight of Diana's ashen face and putting a kettle of water on to boil that would make uncountable cups of tea. "I had a million adventures when I was a kid. Would you believe that Madelaine never had one? Did I ever tell you about the time…" Her chatter seemed to go on and on through the swirling, storming hours, and Diana merely caught snatches of the dialogue. Her real attention was focused on the terrifying happenings outside. She was, nevertheless, grateful for her aunt's presence.

It was nearly 5:00 a.m. when in the black, dripping stillness that followed the violence of the storm, Diana heard the roar of Ross's truck in the drive, the sound of wheels crunching into the shell drive.

Diana ran to the door and threw it open, her long black hair streaming over her shoulders. Then she plunged outside, not caring when wet shell and gum balls bit into her bare feet. "Ross…Adam… Is he…"

The words died away in her throat as the youthful, vibrant voice of her son called her name. He stretched toward her from the open window of the cab. "Mother…"

She opened the door on the passenger side of the

truck and flung her arms about her little boy, burying her face against the woodsy damp of his jacket. The frozen wall about her heart seemed to melt, and she was instantly flooded with a warm tide of relief and love and gratitude. Her shining eyes lifted to Ross's and met his cold, bleak stare. There was a remoteness to him, an indifference in the chiseled cast of his bronzed features, that at first she didn't understand.

Tears coursed down her face. She had been so wrong...so foolishly wrong to behave toward him as she had. Why had she driven him away like that, as though he were nothing to her? She reached for his hand, wanting to make up to him for the way she had behaved, wanting to beg him to forgive her. But he drew his fingers from hers as though he'd touched fire and painfully burned. He stepped out of the truck, proud and alone, and lifted Adam down.

"Ross...I...I'm sorry."

"*I'm sorry*'s aren't going to get it this time. I told you how I felt before I left," he said tersely, turning abruptly from her so that all she saw was the squared broadness of his back and shoulders as he strode rapidly toward the house carrying Adam.

"Ross..."

Brutally he ignored the fragile sound, and she remembered his words, *You and I are finished....*

Her world crashed in around her.

Ten

Her fingertip looped idly through the handle of what must have been her seventh cooling cup of her Aunt Patricia's tea. Diana stared hopelessly up into the coldly set, handsome features of her husband. Why didn't Aunt Patricia just leave him alone?

"Of course I know what I'm doing, Patricia. I want her gone tomorrow," Ross stated, finality in his tone, his voice deliberately cool.

He might as well not have spoken, for Patricia always refused to listen to what she didn't want to hear. "But that's so ridiculous, dear," she began, ignoring his ominous frown as well as the tightening of his jawline. She poured herself a fourteenth cup of tea despite her feeling of fullness, despite the very real sensation that she was washing away from having drunk so much of it. "The two of you were made for each other, and as I see it, from a doctor's point of view, the situation is really quite simple and quite...quite salvageable."

"I don't give a damn for your doctor's point of view or for anything else you have to say on the subject," Ross snarled. "You're poking your nose into my life with that same gleam in your eye Madelaine always has."

"Now, *that* cut!" Patricia did indeed look miffed to be so unfavorably compared to her sister. "Madelaine wants to break you up."

"For the first time in my acquaintance with her we're in agreement," Ross snapped.

"You don't really mean that, Ross dear. Your male ego has suffered a blow because Diana rejected you again in the same manner she did when Tami died, but that's no reason to end a marriage."

"Can't you understand," he said wearily at last, as though he didn't care in the least whether she did or not, "that there's more to it than that. She isn't there for me when the chips are down. I want a woman who can stand by me, not someone who turns on me when I need her the most."

"That's a perfectly reasonable way to feel about one's wife," Patricia agreed.

"Good!" he said. "I'm glad you see things my way."

"Oh, I wouldn't say that. I want you two back together."

"Dream on, and while you do I'm going to bed. This has been one hell of a night."

"There's something the two of you don't know," Patricia began, "that will clear this whole unfortunate matter up, something I should have told Diana years ago...but was too afraid of Madelaine to do."

Ross was stalking toward the door when Diana's soft reply to her aunt stopped him. "It's no use, Aunt Patricia. He's too stubborn and hardheaded to listen to anyone once his mind is made up."

Ross whirled toward her, his eyes blazing. "The hell I am!" His angry gaze met and held Diana's gentle one, and for her it was as if an electrical charge surged through her before he ripped his eyes away. "Well, go ahead," he ground out through clenched teeth, as stubbornly intent on hearing what Patricia had to say as he had been on leaving only seconds before.

"I think there's a very good reason that Diana froze you out and thereby precipitated both crises in your marriage. She was adopted. I placed her myself in my sister's home when she was two and a half years old. I promised Madelaine that I would never tell anyone this, and I've stuck by my promise until now. However, I can't stand by and let this secret wreck three lives."

"Adopted..." Diana murmured as a million unanswered questions swirled in her mind while at the same time so many lifelong mysteries were instantly solved. Who was she and where had she come from? But at last she knew why she'd always felt she had to try so hard to please her mother, why it was so important to be perfect and to win approval. She understood the strange alienation she felt in her parents' house, as though she didn't really quite belong, as well as her fervent desire to adopt Adam and make him feel wanted when she'd married Ross. She remembered how Madelaine could never bring herself to touch or caress her. Relief washed through her at this new and unexpected self-understanding. But what did any of this have to do with Ross?

"What the hell could that possibly have to do with anything?" Ross muttered, though a strange curiosity was invading his own consciousness as he looked at his wife, his expression frankly speculative, the line of his jaw less stubborn looking.

"I think it all hinges on the tragedy that separated Diana from her natural parents," Patricia began slowly. "When she was two her parents took her on a camping trip in Colorado, and during a mountain storm, a tree limb fell on their tent, killing her parents instantly. A day later the poor child—Diana—was found toddling about in the forest all alone and crying. She was completely terrified. Apparently the storm had awakened her, and she had disobeyed her parents and had wandered out of the tent in the night—just in the nick of time. I think in her immature mind she thought the accident happened because she hadn't minded, as some sort of punishment...that she deserved. She kept saying over and over, 'My fault...my fault....'"

"How dreadful," Ross murmured. A new compassion filled his eyes as he went to his wife and stood behind the back of Diana's chair, then slipped his arm about her shoulders.

"Of course," Patricia continued, "we can only speculate now, but I think Diana locked all these feelings away and they surfaced again more powerfully than ever when Tami died. She couldn't remember what had happened to her on a conscious level, but she has never really forgotten...if you know what I mean. She knew that she'd felt like that before. She was understandably baffled and terrified. What I can't fathom is why Madelaine didn't tell you all this then."

"I never tried to explain any feelings about Tami to Mother. They just seemed so strange, and I felt so weird. You know Mother doesn't have any patience when it comes to things like that."

"I was in general practice back then," Patricia said by way of explanation. "One of my patients was the woman who was taking care of you. She had a houseful of children and was only a distant relative of your mother's, Diana, and didn't really think she would be able to care for another child. Madelaine was heartbroken at the time because she had been told that she could never bear children of her own. You can guess the rest."

"Yes...." Diana murmured.

"I think the reason Diana blamed you for Tami, Ross, was that she had to blame someone other than herself for what happened—because she couldn't deal with the intense guilt that would have resulted had she blamed herself. She was afraid of those feelings because they had overwhelmed her once before, when she was a child. Perhaps now you can understand why she's inclined to be so overprotective.''

"Of course I can,'' he said, his tone gentle.

Patricia observed them both long and carefully, and her face relaxed at what she saw. "Well, I think it's time for me to stop playing marriage counselor and go back to Madelaine's house. She may kick me out in the street when she finds out I spilled the beans.''

"I think Mother and I will discover a new and more honest way to understand each other,'' Diana said softly, feeling the deepest gratitude toward her aunt. "Tell her I love her, that nothing could change that or the fact that she is truly my mother.''

Diana turned toward Ross and smiled up into his eyes. She would think about her adoption and what it meant later. Now she wanted to concentrate on her husband.

When Patricia had gone, Ross pulled Diana into his arms. "I think I'll keep you after all,'' he muttered fiercely against her ear, his lips moving beneath the thickly flowing tresses of her hair in a warm nuzzling motion that sent dizzying sensations down the length of her spine. "If you'll have me…after I acted like a blind, arrogant fool, trying to throw you out when you were justifiably terrified about Adam. It was just my own damned guilt.…''

"You can be awfully arrogant…when you think you're in the right,'' she purred teasingly, as though she were actually considering not taking him back. "Ross..." She wanted to tell him how much she loved him, but somehow she couldn't find the words. But her face was aglow, and he saw the depth of her feelings in her eyes.

He crushed her against his chest. The hard force of his body against hers shattered her with an intense, radiant joy. The fear that he had been lost to her made their emotional reunion all the sweeter.

"I thought I'd lost you," she said weakly.

"I was behaving a trifle melodramatically," he admitted sheepishly. "I could never have lived without you." His lips found hers in a kiss that was slow and sensual, arousing and deepening until he gained the wanton response he was seeking.

He lifted his mouth from hers, an intense look of love shining in his eyes. Diana's heart skipped a beat at the sight of gentle emotion on such a powerful man's face. A turbulent flooding of feelings deluged her as she savored his lingering gaze.

"I love you, Diana," he whispered. "I want you with me forever."

"In spite of my...faults and all my stupid mistakes?..."

"Yes." He was smiling broadly down at her, his eyes adoring every beautiful feature. "There are some differences between us that we can never change— and I'll have to teach you to drive properly, of course, even if it takes the rest of my life...which it probably will."

"You're just like a big old lion with a cowardly

streak—when it comes to cars. I already know how to drive," she insisted stubbornly.

"About as well as Adam at that go-cart track he's so crazy about," Ross teased. "I'll even move into town now that I understand why you don't like the forest."

"Now I know you love me." She was beaming smugly.

"I always have."

"I'm not afraid of the forest anymore, since I know the reason for my feelings. This is home, and I never want to move," she said almost shyly.

"Neither do I...as long as you're here. Welcome home, my darling." There was commitment and the deepest kind of love in his voice.

"We'll never be able to agree on everything," she said. "We're too different. There will always be problems...."

"Yes, but we'll find a way to work them out."

"Ross, there is one thing..."

"What, honey?"

"Who's Linda?"

"Jealous?" When she nodded, he smiled broadly. "Good, it's your turn—after the way you tortured me with that older and so-very-debonair multimillionaire of yours."

"You didn't answer my question," she whispered, her heart filling with doubt.

"She's just a good friend," he explained softly, his expression amused.

"Nothing else?"

"You should know me well enough by now to know I'm a one-woman man." The disturbing intensity of his gold eyes meeting hers didn't waver, and she saw the truth.

Ross kissed her forehead, then lightly trailed a kiss down to the upturned velvet-softness of her lips. Easily he lifted her into his arms.

"Where are you taking me?" she queried breathlessly.

"To our bedroom."

"Up those stairs?"

"Just like *Gone With the Wind*."

"Oh, Ross...." Her fingers tightened around the corded hardness of his neck muscles.

"You know what I wish?" he asked, carrying her through the den as though she were as light as a wisp of down.

"What?"

"That we had a swing up there like the one you have in Houston. That was the damnedest night in my life." He chuckled, and his eyes lit with the pleasantly erotic memory. "You know that, don't you?"

"It was meant to be. I knew then I wanted you back, Ross. I wanted so much for you to love me again."

"And as always, you got your way...my spoiled little rich girl. And I intend to keep on spoiling you." His gaze drifted warmly over her like an intimate caress.

"And I, you. Did you know...for your birthday

present I'm going to order a swing for our bedroom here?''

He paused on the landing, adjusting her body against his, smiling tenderly down at her. ''We may have to raise the ceiling to get it in there, but I'd almost be agreeable to tearing the house down if it came to that.''

Forceful strides carried her into the bedroom, where he laid her down in the middle of the bed. He stood there with the light of the golden dawn flooding the room and stared down at her with desire making his beautiful, black-lashed eyes seem even more golden than ever before. Then the bed dipped with his muscular weight, and they were kissing each other deeply, as though they could never get enough of each other. Her hands fumbled at the buttons of his shirt until they parted, and she could feel the heat of naked flesh beneath her shaking hands.

She loved him so desperately. She just hadn't known it for a while. And to think how close she'd come to losing him. Tears of happiness brimmed beneath her thick dark lashes. His hands were undressing her and his lips followed the path of his hands, caressing the soft skin along her neck, nibbling lower, ever lower to kiss her nipples until they were erect, roseate buds of desire, lowering his hot, probing mouth still lower, past the erogenous area of her navel to explore the exquisite, vulnerable womanliness of her, his black head buried in her yielding softness.

She was his and he was hers, and in the burning light of a new sun they surrendered to the white-hot heat of their love, reveling in the wanton splendor of lips so hot they scorched like fire, of passions so intensely turbulent they could do nothing but let them wash over their bodies in a great flaming tide of loving desire.

* * * * *

SPECIAL EDITION

Stories of love and life, these powerful novels are tales that you can identify with— romances with "something special" added in!

Fall in love with the stories of authors such as **Nora Roberts, Diana Palmer, Ginna Gray** and many more of your special favorites—as well as wonderful new voices!

Special Edition brings you entertainment for the heart!

SSE-GEN

SILHOUETTE®
Desire®

Do you want...

Dangerously handsome heroes

Evocative, everlasting love stories

Sizzling and tantalizing sensuality

Incredibly sexy miniseries like **MAN OF THE MONTH**

Red-hot romance

Enticing entertainment that can't be beat!

You'll find all of this, and much *more* each and every month in **SILHOUETTE DESIRE**. Don't miss these unforgettable love stories by some of romance's hottest authors. Silhouette Desire—where your fantasies will always come true....

DES-GEN

♥ *Silhouette* ROMANCE™

What's a single dad to do when he needs a wife by next Thursday?

Who's a confirmed bachelor to call when he finds a baby on his doorstep?

How does a plain Jane in love with her gorgeous boss get him to notice her?

From classic love stories to romantic comedies to emotional heart tuggers, **Silhouette Romance** offers six irresistible novels every month by some of your favorite authors! Such as...beloved bestsellers **Diana Palmer, Annette Broadrick, Suzanne Carey, Elizabeth August** and **Marie Ferrarella**, to name just a few—and some sure to become favorites!

Fabulous Fathers...Bundles of Joy...Miniseries... Months of blushing brides and convenient weddings... Holiday celebrations... You'll find all this and much more in **Silhouette Romance**—always emotional, always enjoyable, always about love!

SR-GEN